THE KEEPER

THE HUNT FOR THE SOUTH LONDON SERIAL KILLER

NINA BLACK

BLOODHOUND
— BOOKS —

For Harry, Betsy and Clare with grateful thanks for your help

'Murder is born of love, and love attains the greatest intensity in murder.'

— **Octave Mirbeau**

SATURDAY JULY 15TH, 1995

CHAPTER ONE

DI JO POLLITT

The morning heat is already starting to swell as I run from my house to the Golf parked on the road outside. I jump in, start up and drive fast as I can to Lambeth, fortunately not far from Kennington. I love this car. I bought her second-hand five years ago and then she was four years old though with low mileage. She's proved so reliable and, touch wood, has never once broken down on me.

I straight away call Tony Smith on the mobile phone, thanking my lucky stars I remembered it at the last minute. Egg on face if the inspector turned up without it. They were only issued to us a couple of months ago and I'm still trying to get used to owning this miraculous new gadget.

The sleeping DS answers with a startled grunt. I give him the drift of what's happened and tell him to get himself to the street address soon as. He happens to live in Lambeth so he'll probably be there quicker than I.

I grapple a Camel from my bag, light up with the Zippo, the first of the day and take a few deep drags. My watch reads 5.14am. Although I couldn't feel less like it at this hour, I chuck the unfinished cigarette out of the window and force myself to eat a couple of overripe bananas grabbed from the fruit bowl on my way out. They should have been binned a couple of days ago and taste like mushy cotton wool but there was no time for breakfast. It's shaping up to be a long day ahead and I don't do well on an empty stomach.

I did manage to brush my teeth in ten seconds and to brush my hair. In the rear mirror, I can see it's already doing its own thing and has reverted to an uncontrolled brown mop. Thick and wiry, it has never done as it is told. I examine bleary green eyes for sand. A fingernail does the job.

When I arrive at the scene, a few what I take to be Jamaicans with hanging heads are already gathered on the pavement of the narrow, grimy street. The area has been cordoned off and a tent hides a body.

As predicted, young Tony has got there before me. He lumbers over to where I pull up. I get out and he looks me in the eyes with his big, dark, warm ones, 'Morning, ma'am. Not a pretty sight, I warn you.'

'Thanks, Tony. Murders seldom are.'

'Yes, but this one...' he mumbles and looks away.

A man who could be taken for a heavyweight boxer, Tony looks comical in the white scene suit, mask, gloves and overshoes. It's the hood that simply doesn't suit his big round face. Not, I know very well, that I'll look any better myself. I'm almost the same height as him, if considerably less chunky. You'd call me lanky or long-limbed, whereas large or burly describes Tony Smith.

Reliable, steady and likeable, DS Tony Smith is a through-and-through good man and I'm comfortable working with him. He is loved by all at the station for his fearless determination to bring criminals to justice; his cheerful, happy, get-to-it attitude and his squeaky, high-pitched chortles of laughter that sound like a small child choking and giggling at the same time. In a thousand years no one would believe such a laugh could emanate from such a huge bloke.

The police received a 999 call from a woman at just before 4.30am to report that her husband Winston Clarke hadn't arrived home from work. This call was followed about quarter of an hour later by another reporting a man dead on the pavement close to the block of flats where he lived. A shocked resident leaving the flats had recognised the man and called the police. Because the killing had happened so near to his home, news has spread like wildfire around the community, hence the gathering of people outside.

Winston was a thirty-four-year-old who worked as a bus driver. Having finished his night shift at 3.10am, he dropped his vehicle at the bus depot in Waterloo and walked back, as he did every night, to his home in Lambeth.

Tony hands me some PPE into which I struggle before I bend to enter the tent. The dead man is lying on his back in an awkward position, his legs splayed. A deep, livid mark around the neck indicates he has been garrotted and has died from strangulation. The trousers and underpants have been pulled down to the knees to expose the genitals which have been cut around and detached from the body. Blood has soaked the groin area, extended under the legs, seeped across the pavement and dripped onto the street. As Tony warned, it is not a pretty sight.

My immediate thought is a gang-related killing. In this neighbourhood, just about all the murders are. A man murdered at that time of night in this place is always going to be suspected of involvement with the drugs gangs. Might the emasculation be a new warning to others not to mess with one particular gang? It is possible. Yet the man is not dressed to type and certainly doesn't look like a druggie. Besides, he's a bus driver – an unlikely candidate for being part of a gang.

Liz Watts is kneeling beside the corpse, a mask covering her nose and mouth as she works. Considering her job, the pathologist is a surprisingly jolly woman. While others are combing the area for clues, she is surrounded by a cloud of flies. I know whose job I'd prefer.

'Hello there. Thought you'd retired, Liz?'

She stands up to greet me. I am conscious that, like many females and a number of men, she feels diminished when she stands next to me. I've become used to this over the years. At times its consequences stand me in good stead and at others work against me, in particular with certain men who feel belittled and can turn a tad aggressive to compensate.

'Hello Jo, circumstances aside, it's nice to see you. You are correct; I have indeed retired and am only standing in for the new man who's on holiday for a couple of weeks.'

'Ah, I see. Enjoying retirement, I trust?'

'I am indeed, but happy to return from time to time.' She flashes a brief smile before returning her gaze to the corpse.

'Funny one we've got here. Highly unusual. Very nasty thing but mercifully, it appears the mutilation happened after death, which would have been the quickest. Hopefully, I can tell you more once we get him back to the morgue.'

'Any sign of the genitals?'

She shakes her head. 'Not so far.'

A thorough police search of the scene finds no trace of the amputated parts. Has the murderer planned to do something with them? Or have they simply disposed of them? In either case, why? I contemplate these thoughts with disgust.

There are many angles to think about. Winston was older and more ordinary than the younger drug dealers; and the usual gang killings were stabbings or shootings, not strangulations and certainly not castrations.

CHAPTER TWO

'Can I help?' he said.

It was hard to see on the dark side street and he peered forward to read the piece of paper before it fluttered out of my hand to the pavement.

Without waiting for the answer, he bent down to pick it up... the kind of man he was. The sort who would always help out where he can. A man I felt relieved to have chosen. Before he had even grasped hold of the scribbled map, the cord had slipped over his head and tightened around his neck; his head had been yanked back; and my knee was thrusting deep into his back.

His throat constricted when I twisted as tight as I was able. When he jerked backward attempting a scream, no sound emerged except a faint gurgle as the larynx crushed against the back of the throat. The knot had done its job.

His strong, stocky body threshed and flailed for what seemed only seconds before he slowly buckled and crumpled. He was heavy and dropped with a thud as life leached from him fast.

I crouched in front of his distorted body lying on the

pavement on that hot, muggy London night and swiftly but carefully removed what he was well rid of and wouldn't be needing anymore.

My heart was racing and I'm not ashamed to admit to myself that I was somewhat scared as well as excited. The sensation felt like that time long ago when the police found me alone in the car.

I have to say I am proud of the speed and of the neat job I made of it, even though I was in a hurry. I'll admit I was extremely nervous about the whole thing. He was fairly short but bigger and stronger than I had intended for my first and I wasn't at all sure my strength was going to be up to it. But it worked and I succeeded.

And it felt so, so good. Both worse and better by far than I ever could have imagined. Exhilarating, nerve-racking, terrifying and wonderful.

At last, it's done. I have wondered about this for so long that now I can hardly believe it has happened. Mamma would have been proud of me. She always said I could do anything I put my mind to.

CHAPTER THREE

DI JO POLLITT

There is nothing for me to do until the family liaison officer arrives. Watching the pathologist at work, I ponder this unusual killing.

A weird MO that poses an unusual set of questions. First of all, the motive: revenge, rage or jealousy? I feel all three can be ruled out as there is no obvious anger about the killing. It is neat and careful.

Then there is the next question: was the victim known to the killer? I think he possibly may have been, which raises further questions.

Did a member or friend of the family commit the murder on behalf of the wife? Had Winston been playing away? Had the wife wanted rid of her husband for some other reason? Did someone else have another reason to be rid of him – but if so, was the motive sexual jealousy? Were they after the wife?

I need to meet and talk to Mrs Clarke soon as. I check my pocket to feel for my little bottle of herbal calming remedy. I use it in particularly stressful situations. Whether or not it is a placebo doesn't bother me. For me it works. A few drops on the tongue always helps me tackle the direst of situations and I take some now.

At about 7.40, the female family liaison officer turns up and accompanies me and Tony as we head to the flat entrance to interview Sandrene Clarke. Tony is Jamaican himself, so he knows how to handle himself around this area. Many of his compatriots frown on him for joining the pigs but he stands his ground. He also copes well with the institutionalised racism within the force itself.

It's a typical red-brick seventies-built council block of flats in Lambeth in which there are six floors and about forty flats. The air thick with marijuana, the odd syringe abandoned in the corridors, spliff butts littering the dark staircases. We find our way up the dirty concrete flights of steps to the fifth floor where the Clarkes' flat is.

Cops are strictly unwelcome here but in a case like this, the residents will make an exception. Winston was evidently popular and for those who don't yet know about the killing, having Tony with us makes us less conspicuous and safer than we might have been without him. Being females in plain clothes helps as well, although these folk can sniff police from a distance.

Sandrene, a shapely woman who must weigh around thirteen stone, opens the door. A head of magnificent bushy hair that from side to side measures a minimum fourteen inches frames a kind, plump face with huge dark eyes that are bloodshot from crying. When she sees us, she starts to howl and throws her arms around Tony's neck who, in spite of his own size briefly staggers under her weight as she shakes and sobs on his shoulder.

Once she has calmed down some, we persuade her to invite us through to her small living room that is full to bursting with her own sizable family and the children of others as well as her own, some of whom have overflowed into the bedrooms.

I employ as much tact as I know when asking them all to leave temporarily so we can talk to the widow in private. The group doesn't look at all happy about this and at one stage it looks as though things might kick off. Fortunately, Sandrene convinces them it's okay to come back in half an hour's time. So, they take her kids and promise to return when she calls them.

At a nod from me, Tony offers to make us coffee and goes quietly into the kitchen. I sit on an armchair facing Sandrene so I can see her face to face. I need to be able to read her expressions carefully while talking to her. The liaison officer sits quietly beside her, a discreet packet of tissues on her lap, ready to comfort the grieving widow and to listen to all that is said.

I like to think I am a sympathetic and sensitive woman who particularly identifies with other females and I ask gently about Winston and why anyone might have wanted him dead.

Sandrene is voluble and talking seems to be helping her deal with the terrible shock she is facing. Between her miserable wails, I gather that everybody loved her Winston, that he had no enemies, that he never hurt a fly, that he had loved his God, his children and his Sandrene.

'Who do you think might have done this, Sandrene?' I try my best to be as soft as I can with the poor, distraught woman.

'How do I know? Who would kill him? Who would kill my husband? Who would do such a thing taking my man, hood and all? You tell me who?'

Her cries are so loud and full of grief they are hard for us to bear. If I'd been able, I'd have broken the news of the murder gently and kept the castration for later to give Sandrene the chance to absorb the blow of hearing about her husband's death before facing the brutal details. But she already knows them. No doubt, the family has talked of nothing else. At least we are spared the agony of telling her what had happened to him after his death.

She is concerned that the children know the worst of it as well. I am, too, and make a mental note to self to have a word with the super about keeping the grisly part about the castration out of the papers for the meantime. But with the gossip already everywhere locally it seems unlikely we stand a chance.

By the time we leave Sandrene with the FLO, who she seems to like and respect, I am certain Winston's wife is devastated by her man's loss. I shall interview her again but doubt we'll get any further. It is fairly plain she has no idea who might have done or even had a part in the deed. It seems highly improbable she was involved in any hanky-panky with another and the only way we can find out more about Winston will be from asking around.

By now, I don't believe the murder was gang-related but will have to wait for the autopsy to tell whether there were drugs in Winston's body.

I only know a little about garrottes and what I don't, I shall look up later. An easy-to-conceal, rapid, silent and deadly way of killing, approaching the victim from behind, the killer slips the garrotte over their victim's head and around their necks before, generally with the aid of a knee in the back, they yank the person backward while twisting the cord or wire to tighten it causing death by asphyxiation.

***

Later in the day, the heat and humidity mounts and the city perspires. Everyone trying to work longs to finish and go home to a cold bath or shower; or simply to sleep. Dark clouds and rumbles of thunder tantalise with the hope that a storm will break and clear the air. But the threat never materialises, the heaviness continues and people feel tired and irritable. Me too.

Once Liz Watts has had time to examine the victim, we take a Fiesta from the car pool and Tony and I join her at the mortuary. I don't blanch at the sight of dead bodies these days. Unfortunately, I've seen too many.

Tony, on the other hand, can't bear to look. He has to avert his eyes and looks as though he might throw up, but then he is male. The body is still unopened but naked and the large wound where the genitals are missing is unsettling for anyone to see. The neutered corpse looks unreal as it waits on the metal table for others to decide its future after such an indecent release from life.

We stand uncomfortably around the body. I ask for an approximate time of death and Liz replies, 'Somewhere between 0330 and 0500, but if you pushed me, I'd put it between 0330 and 0430.'

Pointing to the dark welt across the neck, she continues, 'I found some fine white cotton cord fibres embedded in and around here. There is some deep lividity in particular over the area of the larynx where, from the depressions in the surrounding tissue I have been able to establish that the strangulation was caused by cord that had been knotted in the middle. Incorporated to crush the larynx, I presume.

'This means that the killer successfully disabled the vocal cords in order to make the kill as soundless as possible, apart perhaps from a few faint gurgles. Knowing how to kill with a garrotte is one thing but to know how to place the thing around the neck at the correct spot to crush the larynx in this manner means this killer is not only clever but possibly trained.

'Also, the genitals had been removed by slicing through the

surrounding flesh in two clean cuts. No slasher at work here. This is no angry, vicious attack.' She pauses and beckons to an assistant to come and help her turn the cadaver over. As they do so, she murmurs, 'A strange murder, this. There appears to have been no sexual interference with the body and no other wound apart from the strangulation. No blood under the fingernails and no signs of any struggle. There are no fingerprints or any other human evidence traced on the remains. Whoever killed this man was extremely careful. There is one thing though.' She points to the victim's back. 'A large contusion was found here corresponding to a cluster of minute black PVC fibres I found on the middle of the back of the T-shirt.'

'PVC? In this weather? God!'

'Yes, I was surprised too.'

'But the bruise is no surprise. To put additional pressure on the neck, as is common in the case of a garrotte being used, a murderer often plants a knee in the victim's back to help to thrust the body forward and jerk the head back to enable a swift, and in this case soundless, death.'

'So the killer kneed the guy in the back while strangling him to get a better hold? And the killer's knee was encased in black plastic.'

Liz looks at me. 'Looks like it.'

We discuss it further and decide that if the fibres do not belong to apparel, then they might belong to a plastic cover used to prevent blood getting onto the killer's clothes. But Liz Watts' careful measurements show that an average adult knee would fit the bruise exactly. Makes no sense at all. Black PVC trousers, surely not?

The pathologist has examined the stomach contents and tested the blood for traces of illegal substances, of which none have been found. As I thought, the drug connection is looking less likely by the minute. I wonder whether this murderer has killed before. I ask myself what people are trained in such matters. SAS? Espionage? I resolve to check back over cases during the past ten years to see if any similar murders or attempted murders come up. I will also check to ensure that Winston wasn't working as some sort of agent... unlikely, but you never know.

Thanking Liz, we head back to the police station in Southwark. Once we get there, I leave Tony to park the car while I walk back into the big old 1940s red-brick police station and head to my office where photos have already been left on my desk. I sit down and leaf through them. Gruesome they are. I pick three, one close-up of the face and neck, one of Winston's entire body and a third of the wound where the genitals have been sliced away.

I take the prints and make my way to the major incident room. Having wound through the layers of officers at their desks to the end of the room and over to the whiteboard, I pin up the close-up photos of Winston's vandalised body. A lot of the faces are looking up at the pictures as I return to my office to report by phone to the superintendent.

He asks me to come to his office. Since becoming detective chief superintendent, Maurice Green has changed. Lately, he seems to care more and more about the fact that he is in charge. I suppose being bound to a desk, as well as not being far from retiring must be the reason. Too much time to think, has old Maurie.

'Nasty business, this one. Let's get this bloody killer caught quickly, Jo. It's already in the early edition of the *Standard*. Pity the bloody press had to get hold of it. Did you take any steps to withhold some of the more, as they would see it, appetising details?'

'I've had no chance. Just about the whole of Lambeth knew about it before we did.'

'Pity. Any leads so far?'

'No prints, no DNA, nothing to go on apart from some fibres. A very careful murderer. We're on the case, I can assure you, Maurie.'

'Right.' A terse tone and unusually for him, he doesn't look at me. 'I want to be kept informed of your every step, Pollitt,' and he waves me away.

Pollitt, not *Jo,* and he hasn't looked at me. It's then I realise he wants me to call him 'Sir'.

Generally unworried by protocol, I'm not bothered about the super's reaction. Catching criminals concerns me; not kow-towing to the boss or how fellow officers perceive me. After all, I know Maurie so well and I've worked with him a long time. We were DSs together and then DIs.

Silly old bugger, I think, *he can't really care about such nonsense, can he?*

After a laborious search by a large team of police officers, no similar murder is discovered in police records. Not a single one. Lambeth, indeed London, has a new kind of killer. The motive is out there somewhere.

Back home in Kennington, I feel exhausted. It's been a very long day. I call the cats who come running for their supper. They wrap themselves around my legs, gazing up at me and mewing loudly while I find a new tin of cat food in one of the kitchen cupboards and scrape the contents into their bowls.

Ginger makes his usual attack on the food as though ravenous and gulps his down too fast in order to push Blackie away and steal his before he has finished. Poor Blackie never learns to eat faster and always allows this to happen.

The ill-fated Winston had no chance to put up a fight. He was strong and had he done so he might still be alive now. But his killer, like Ginger, was an opportunist who slipped in and took his chance before his victim even knew what was happening.

Not much in the freezer appropriate for this weather, so I am left with the choice of fish fingers or a shepherd's pie. I choose the latter and slip it into the oven. While this is heating, my time arrives. I take a full ice tray from the freezer compartment of the fridge and make myself my summertime cocktail.

I have a wonderful cocktail shaker kit that was bought for me by my best pal Cilla Pelham when I was made a DI and I am inordinately proud of it. I used to manage with a plastic jug with a lid on it, which was not at all the same.

In the autumn, I go for Bloody Marys and in colder weather, Baileys White Russians. But in hot weather a Cosmopolitan is my homecoming ritual, my special unwinding me-time and I love it. A mix of flavours that, in my opinion, blend together to make a thing of beauty.

First, I fill the shaker half full of ice then add two measures of vodka, one of Grand Marnier, two small measures of cranberry juice. Then I squeeze the juice of two limes on top. I shake the cocktail for about thirty seconds until the drink is well chilled. For an extra burst of flavour, I peel a twist of orange peel over the filled cocktail glass and garnish it with that. This way, the orange oils spray into the glass.

Just to look at such a beautiful colour as the liquid has become always cheers me up, even when I'm on a murder investigation. I take a large sip before I go through to the living room to sit myself on the sofa, place the glass on the table beside the settee and call Cilla as I do every evening. We agreed some time ago that I'd be the one to call since my hours are so unpredictable.

Cilla and I became best pals in the sixth form at school and have remained so ever since. She had recently moved locally from another London district, I was never sure why. Neither one of us has married or had kids. We both love our jobs as much as we love each other. I suppose we just don't feel the need for anyone else in our personal lives, mainly because we have so little time left over for ourselves and all we seem to need is one another. We even holiday together. It's always been that way since we were children, when we played happily together during school and holidays, and I'm sure it always will be.

In some ways we are extremely similar. Both of us are tall and strong, both committed to our jobs, both not particularly concerned with finding a man. In fact, those times have long gone when we used to think we should have boyfriends. We both did for a time, but they didn't work out. Both of us had bad fathers. Hers died when she was young, while mine scarpered, so we share the experience of being brought up by single mums.

We both try to keep in shape – at least that is when we get the chance. Actually Cilla does a lot more than me and trains in a gym twice a week. She lifts weights and rides static bikes and walks on treadmills and bounces about on giant balls. She's super fit and cycles to work and everywhere around London. We love long country walks when we can find the time and are never bored with each other's company.

We recently discovered our new craze of cocktails and when we're free, love to go out to a cocktail bar on a Friday or Saturday night before having a meal at a pub somewhere. Perhaps I love the cocktails a bit more than Cilla, but then I reckon my job is that much more stressful and there is nothing like a cocktail or four to alleviate stress.

Cilla's beautiful in a quirky kind of way. Long blonde hair and bluey-green eyes but a hell of a long way from any Barbie doll. Her nose was broken from a fall when she was about fifteen and she has a charming bump in it and she wears spectacles which make her look more serious than she actually is.

Having said we are similar we are also quite different in other ways. I think I am more highly strung than Cilla, who I would say is down to earth and practical as well as efficient. She is clever and did better than me in maths and science at school, as well as creative skills such as art and drama, while I scored high in English, history and, later when I went to uni, in sociology and psychology. I suppose you could say we were both clever-clogs at school which helped us bond together as clever-clogs never tend to be too popular with the others.

I sip the delicious drink, holding the cordless handset between my left shoulder and chin while she asks how my day went and I don't tell her about the murder. It will take too long and I just don't have the energy for questions and answers now: I'm too tired to do anything except to drink, eat and go to sleep.

Cilla, who knows me better than anyone – except Mum who knew me best – says she can hear how exhausted I sound and that she imagines I must have worked on a hard case today. She is fishing and probing and guessing that something worse than the usual bad day for a detective inspector has occurred.

I admit that it has been an arduous day but still don't bite... I just don't want to discuss it now. She even asks if there's been a murder but finally gives up and tells me to look after myself, have a couple of Cosmos and get some kip as early as possible.

It's not as though Cilla doesn't have a busy job too. As a veterinary nurse, she is frequently late, assisting as she does in major operations on animals. At other times she will stay overnight at the surgery where they have a bed for a nurse to give night care to any animals that need it. There's a rota and she'll take her turn, which she did last night.

Deeply committed to animal care, as a child Cilla always adored animals and used to say she wanted to be a vet. But so do a number of kids. She was the one who stuck to her guns. As she grew older, she decided she didn't have the stomach to perform life-saving surgery on a dying animal as she felt she couldn't trust herself emotionally.

So instead of training as a vet, she studied to be a nurse. She has discovered over time that this is just as gruelling. But she has developed a thicker skin and now that she's in her early forties she can trust herself to distance herself from caring too much when an animal fails to survive. She knows she has done her best and that that is all she can do. We have both had to learn the hard way to grow crocodile hides.

I say goodnight, take a large gulp of my drink, stretch out my legs, throw my head back on the sofa, close my eyes and feel Blackie jump onto my knee. When you stroke him, however half-heartedly, he will always reward with his own special purr. The more you stroke the louder he purrs. If you keep on, he will crescendo gradually to incorporate new sounds that include a faint rattle, the occasional back-of-the-throat squeak and even a kind of chirruping vibrato that usually gets me giggling. But this evening there is no comfort to be had. In spite of the drink I cannot escape feeling tired and glum.

The inescapable fact is that I miss Mum terribly. As I think it, I feel the familiar cold stab at my heart and the flash of virulent anger that always accompanies it. Then the tears come. They sting and escape from my closed eyes. Cross with myself, I wipe them away but more follow. I am overtired, I know. We all have less resistance to emotion when overtired.

I ask myself, will this feeling ever let up? One day, will I become used to what has happened? One day, will I get over it?

Will I stop wishing I could see her face, her smile, hear her greeting when I come home? Will I stop longing to talk to her? Wanting to laugh with her? Ever stop simply wishing she wasn't dead?

The grief I live through is sometimes overpowering and the only way I find to cope with it is to keep busy. Whenever I stop, a waterfall of pain drenches me in a deluge that takes my feet from under me, threatens to carry me away and drown me in sorrow.

Cosmo gone, I return to the kitchen and grapple with myself for a few seconds before deciding not to have another. I must be on form tomorrow – it'll be a busy one.

The shepherd's pie is ready so I get it out, find a knife, fork and plate and sit down to eat it with some tomatoes, lettuce, a bit of sliced cucumber and salad cream at the old yellow Formica-topped kitchen table.

Opposite the table on the wall next to a picture of my lovely mum when she was young, is a sepia, framed photograph of her parents. My grandfather stands stiffly in his best suit which is quite a bit too large for him. Under that he sports a white shirt and his best tie while Nanna stands equally straight beside him staring directly at the camera and looking uncomfortable in a white ankle-length frock, with two-inch-heeled slightly pointy shoes, broad straps across the insteps. A sad-looking bunch of ferns and roses hangs from one of her hands on the end of a rigid arm. Both look excruciatingly wooden and unhappy and stare miserably at the camera in front of them.

Nanna actually looks as though Grandad has just farted really badly, while he looks as though he definitely has and is desperate with embarrassment. It is their wedding day.

Mum and I laughed about it so many times, the more so as we knew they were in fact a very happy couple, both of whom loved each other hugely.

I think back to when I was six years old. My father who, from what little I had been able to find out about him, was an incorrigible philanderer, had run away with another woman, leaving my mum alone to raise me with no financial or emotional aid. He vanished from our lives, not even leaving a note to his wife to say he was sorry.

Fortunately for me, the small terraced house I now live in belonged to my maternal grandparents who had taken in their daughter and small child when 'that bugger', as Grandad called him, left.

When I was ten years old, Grandad wasn't there anymore and I was told that he had 'passed'. No one ever mentioned 'that bugger' again. Apart from memories of a cheerful, fun-loving character who cuddled and tickled and made me laugh, that name was all I knew about my father. From thenceforward, my home became an all-female household. My grandmother died soon afterwards of cancer according to the doctor; but of a broken heart according to Mum, so the two of us had been left in the house together.

Having finished my supper, I'm too tired to watch telly so I lock up, call the cats. Ginger is out but faithful Blackie comes to my side, rubs himself against my legs and runs up the stairs ahead of me. Ginger will come through the cat-flap when he wishes.

I have moved into Mum's bedroom. Sleeping in her old double bed helps me to feel closer to her. I leave the door ajar for Ginger.

I fall asleep the moment my head hits the pillow, but by 3am I'm awake again. I roll over and try to go back to sleep, to turn again, disturbing the cats from their positions, one on the pillow next to me, the other on my legs. The horrific sight of Winston Clarke's corpse comes to my mind interspersed with images of my mum's unrecognisable beaten-up face lying on that hospital pillow before she died.

The trial of her killer is taking so, so long to come about. When it finally does, I hope beyond hope that that effing bastard gets the toughest, fiercest, most punitive judge in London. It takes me what seems like an age to get back to sleep but at least I don't wake again until 7am which is when I get up.

JULY 31ST TO DECEMBER 31ST, 1995

CHAPTER FOUR

DI JO POLLITT

Over the days and weeks that follow the Clarke murder, along with Tony I interview Winston's friends, his bosses, co-workers and all who knew him but come up with nothing to suggest he had any enemies at all. Everyone appears to have liked him and he seems to have been a clean-living, church-going man.

The white cotton cord fibres are eventually matched to 5mm cord that is commonly sold for clothes lines. It is widely available to department stores and ironmongery shops and its purchase is to prove impossible to trace.

Our team carries on searching for the murderer but with no evidence, no witnesses and no DNA with which to query the new UK National Criminal Intelligence DNA Database, there is so little to go on. We search for a match to the black PVC fibres but the best we come up with is guesswork.

A brainstorming session with other detectives arrives at the idea of some kind of plastic trousers. Or sheeting, one suggests. But how and why would the killer employ PVC sheeting, someone else says. They all fall silent. None of it makes any sense.

'What about gloves?' a bright spark offers.

'Now you're talking,' another replies.

Since the fibres have been found on the back of the vic's T-shirt, how could the killer have put one of his hands there when both were engaged in garrotting the man?

The distance I appear to keep from my team is deliberately cultivated when working as I understand that when it comes to being in command, familiarity is in danger of breeding contempt. The officers who have known me a long time are well aware of the apparent two-sided nature of their boss and the reason I have adopted this approach.

I tilt my head to one side. 'And do you have any equally clever ideas about where you might be likely to be able to buy a pair of black PVC gloves, sergeant?'

The man's cheeks colour and he hesitates. 'I er, couldn't say exactly, ma'am.' He stumbles over his words and digs himself a bigger hole when he says, 'abroad, perhaps?'

I take a long drag from my cigarette, inhale, raise my eyebrows and allow the smoke gently to drift from my nostrils. There is no need for words. It's an action my team know only too well and it always works. Titters are heard around the room. I calmly study the floor until they all feel discomfited and fall quiet.

They are clutching at absurdly fragile straws and we're getting nowhere fast. I need them to pull themselves together and start thinking straight again. They must concentrate and help me find this killer. That I totally understand and share their frustration is a given. This case looks as though it is going to be a hard nut to crack. I bring the meeting to an abrupt close.

I have plenty of other cases to keep me busy, so for now I get back to them. The major one that is currently taking most of my time is an unusual domestic killing by the elderly sister of her equally elderly brother. We have her in custody but proving that she killed him is not easy. We know she did; but concrete evidence is turning out to be hard to find. And whether it was murder or manslaughter is uncertain.

For weeks and months afterwards we follow every lead, however futile it seems. But we make no progress at all. Exasperation and concern take it in turns to tug at my mind as I have a dire feeling that sooner or later, Winston Clarke's killer plans to repeat his nauseating MO.

FRIDAY JANUARY 5TH TO SATURDAY
JANUARY 6TH, 1996

CHAPTER FIVE

AHMAD HUSSAIN

Having finished his evening shift at 3am, Ahmad Hussain high-fives goodnight to his brother and steps out into the icy night air. He pulls his beanie low over his ears and hugs himself tight in his blue fleece as he turns left out of the shop. It is colder than ever and not only is it freezing but there is a bitter gusty wind that makes it seem even worse. He walks fast to hurry home to some warmth and a hot drink.

Their father is so mean about keeping them heated in the shop, insisting on having the door open in all weathers so that people know they are open. So old-fashioned, the stubborn old goat. He has allowed them to keep an electric radiator in the shop but it is next to useless with the freezing air and wind coming in from outside. The boys have asked him time and again to put a large sign saying OPEN on the door or on a stand-up sign on the pavement but he won't listen. The sleazy club a few doors up closes at 2.30am and a few drunks stagger in for fags and booze but once they've gone hardly any customers come in between 3am and 6am. But their father would rather his sons died of exposure to icy temperatures than risk losing the sale of a packet of Basmati rice or some lentils. They are all too scared of him to argue.

Ahmad has perfected a particular swagger to his walk which he almost forgets but just remembers to put into practice as he moves fast along Upper Tooting Road passing barber shops, cake shops, cafés, Halal butchers and the Job Centre until he turns left down Radenell Road, right along Greenfield then left along Longbrook. Now he moves faster to get home and out of this shit.

The street lighting is poor along these streets but his wicked rubber-soled Reebok InstaPumps that cost him almost three weeks' wages save him when he nearly loses his footing on a frozen puddle on the pavement. Those shoes is sick. He cleans them carefully and regularly. They mean a lot to him.

He thinks about what else he likes and this includes Fatema. His parents approve of her and she has been accepted as a good Muslim girl, but on the wages his father pays him and what Fatema earns helping in her parents' restaurant, they are never going to have enough to move out together. The main problem at the moment though is finding anywhere private to have sex. She is keen on that and he likes her body a lot. Sometimes he can borrow his older brother's scooter and take her out to Wimbledon where they hunt for a quiet spot and do things in the woods.

CHAPTER SIX

I t was freezing cold and hellish windy but I still went out because I could no longer stop myself. In the dark where I waited, across the road I saw him high-five another young man as he left Hussain's 24-hour supermarket and stepped out into the icy night air. He was wearing a beanie and a blue fleece and turned left out of the shop.

He walked fast to hurry home, then, as though he had just remembered, started a particular rolling walk which he put into practice as he moved along Upper Tooting until he turned left. No one to see him, he could now drop the strange walk and move faster after turning left along Longbrook.

He looked just right. Short, on the slim side. Not too hard to handle at all.

That first one was quite burly and I realise I got very lucky there so have decided I must be more cautious in future.

This one was perfect. Excited, I followed well behind. It was so cold. I was wearing thermals. The windchill bit. Not at all the weather for it but the urge had become too strong. I had to... I just had to.

The street lighting was poor along these streets and the

young lad nearly lost his footing on a frozen puddle. He stumbled but picked himself up and after that, aware of the ice in the side streets, he slowed down and walked with more care. I had to watch my step too.

When he turned into the churchyard, my opportunity arose. I called out to him and waved an arm. He stopped and waited for me. Quickly I went up to him and asked my question. Dropped the map; he bent to pick it up. Like magic, it worked again.

I really do have the perfect system. His body would be easy to find soon enough.

I think the whole thing took no more than about ten minutes. How quiet it was. Not a soul about. Just him and me. There was a spirituality in that. There we were. Just the two of us. Me and him. He didn't make a sound in the cold moonlight. We were so close. I watched him expire fast in silence. Lovely clean job. Another one. Good.

I felt ecstatic as I hurried away.

CHAPTER SEVEN

DR EDWARD FLYNN, FORENSIC PATHOLOGIST

The newly appointed Home Office forensic pathologist for Southwark that stretches to include the boroughs of Lewisham, Greenwich and Lambeth has replaced Liz Watts who retired the previous July. In cases of homicide or suspected homicide, forty-one-year-old Doctor Edward Flynn is permanently on call to accompany police to the scene of death. His belief is that one of the greatest mistakes in forensic pathology is failure to attend a scene of crime.

It froze the previous night and is still minus degrees when he reaches the place in Tooting where a murder has occurred. Although it is a star-filled night sky, an icy wind is blowing and conditions are the least hospitable imaginable.

The doctor drives his car and parks on the closest street to the murder scene. It's important to him never to delay in cases of murder. The quicker he can examine a corpse after its demise, the more he can learn and the easier it will be to establish time of death. This is why he always keeps what he calls his 'murder bag' in his car at the ready. In this big, heavy leather case he keeps a waterproof apron, rubber gloves, disposable paper jumpsuits, hair covers, face shields, all the usual GP's things such as thermometer, syringes, et cetera, his autopsy dissection set including handsaw, formalin jars, plastic bags, swabs, foul weather gear – the list goes on.

He gets straight to business.

Standing above the mutilated body, he surveys the scene. The larger majority of blowflies operate in warmer temperatures but certain of them work even in freezing winters. As they always will, through their acute sense of smell, they have found this body within minutes and buzz with excitement around the large open wound.

The scene-of-crime officer is taking photographs and identifying what traces there are available to find. Before anything is moved or even touched, the police have to document everything for their permanent records. In this case there is little to see except bloodstains and some tiny black plastic fibres on the ground. The young victim suffered asphyxiation by means of strangulation.

The pathologist ponders the questions. What position is the body in? What is the state of the victim's clothes? Is there blood? If so, is it spattered and/or pooled? If rigor mortis has started to set in, in what stage is it? Are there any signs of a struggle? Jotting down everything he sees in his notebook, he writes:

Asian male approx 25 – 30. Slight build. Corpse fully clothed on its back, legs slightly splayed, coat open, trousers and pants pulled halfway down thighs to expose missing genitalia. Pooled blood around groin. Deceased before mutilation occurred. No sign semen. Hands/arms clear of marks. No sign of fight/resistance.

CHAPTER EIGHT

DI JO POLLITT

I t's a beautiful starlit night but a cold, cold one and there's a bitter wind. My hair is blowing all over the place. It's not long but it keeps getting in my eyes, which in the darkness makes it hard to see what's going on. I curse my foolishness for having forgotten my beanie in my rush this morning. At least I have some thick gloves which I keep in the Golf, more than those poor chaps in their coveralls do. Latex gloves won't warm hands in this weather.

I approach and introduce myself to the new pathologist.

I tower over him. We greet one another with gloomy faces. It may be our business but it is always a sad occasion to be in the presence of a murder victim. Particularly one as young as this.

When he has finished everything he can do at the scene, the doctor organises men to bag up scrapings of the blood and the fibres. He tells them to cover the body's head, hands and feet in large plastic bags secured with plastic ties as well as the area around the groin which, with difficulty, is sealed to prevent any contamination occurring when they move the body to the mortuary. The men's white coveralls flap in the wind as they work and their hands are freezing.

Later that morning, I arrive with Tony in tow at St George's Hospital mortuary in Tooting where Dr Flynn is working on the body of the young man.

On a cassette recorder, on the shelf of a large bookcase alongside jars of chemicals and other laboratory products, Celine Dion is singing.

Long ago I gave up judging people by their looks or making assumptions on account of their professions; stereotyping doesn't work. I always ask myself questions before drawing conclusions. Is there any reason a forensic pathologist should not play music while he works on a cadaver? The answer must always be a reasoned one.

In this instance, in fact, it seems a calming, even enlightened approach to the work. After all, my dentist, another serious man who is extremely good at his job, always plays pop music while drilling away in readiness for fillings or scraping about looking for trouble among the tombstones.

For a while I watch Dr Flynn at work with his young male assistant. I can see he is a highly diligent worker who will let nothing slip past him. I already feel relieved to have him on side.

'Hello again, Inspector Pollitt. Firstly, may I just say that if you are wondering, as many do, at music being played in a mortuary, I need to say that to my mind, it is the very place for it. I believe ambiance to be important and therefore I make it a habit to play music which I find both soothing to work to, helpful in concentrating the mind and an aid in the emotional disconnect necessary in this business.'

'Please call me Jo, Dr Flynn. I think it is a wonderful idea to lift the atmosphere in such a way.'

'Well, I'm so glad you think so and you must call me Edward.'

A good explanation, I think.

He leans forward over the cadaver, pursing his lips and studying it with a magnifying lens as he continues slowly, 'However, you are not here to discover my taste in music but to find out what I have gleaned from my examination of this young man.'

I watch this middle-aged, dark-haired man and his long, slim, studious face with its slightly aquiline nose bent over the body.

He looks up and says, 'My preliminary findings tell me that Ahmad Hussain is a healthy specimen of a young man in his prime. The lad shows no signs of underlying disease of any sort. No abnormalities, no extraneous wounds, no needle marks, no self-inflicted damage that I can see. He has a tattoo of a naked female on the inside of his left upper thigh which was only noticeable once I had cleaned him up. He is in good shape.'

Tony shuffles on his feet and avoids looking at the corpse. I feel for him as Flynn continues, 'When tested for drugs, I found traces of cannabis in his system. Not surprising. All in all, a normal young man.

'When I looked for fingerprints of another, I found nothing. I searched for trace fibres and came up with the same black PVC plastic ones on his clothing as were, apparently, found on the Lambeth bus driver's body. These were found on the centre back on his fleece jacket where I believe the killer's knee may have been planted.'

So, I say, 'From what you know of it so far, is this looking like a replica killing of the Lambeth bus driver that Dr Watts worked on?'

Flynn nods. 'I would say so, yes.'

I am grateful for the fact that, unlike the scene-of-crime officer, the pathologist does not feel it necessary to point out that this appears to be the work of a serial killer. I also like that, unlike many of them, he graces the victim with his name and talks about him as a real person. So many avoid allowing their corpses to be anything more than that.

'Winston Clarke's death has affected us all,' I say. 'It was such a shocking thing to do to someone who seemed to have been such a well-liked, normal, hard-working family man. A man who had evidently lived for his children and his wife. I was so sorry for the poor wife, who was badly distressed by it. At the time I thought it was less likely to be gang-related than the work of a jealous rival. It didn't cross my mind that it might have been done by a stranger. Of course, all murders are foul but when they are apparently inflicted by a stranger on a stranger, they just make no sense whatsoever.'

Flynn listens carefully. 'Drugs involved, maybe?'

'We searched the man's flat and clothes but there was nothing to indicate that he had any connections with any drug dealer. He was tested in the lab for drugs in his body but nothing showed up.'

Flynn shakes his head in puzzlement.

Police are trained to find answers and when we cannot, it cuts deep.

'One thing that has bothered me about both murders was whether either of them had sexual intercourse with the killer. I know it's a very tricky question to ask as, if this one or both did, any obvious signs have been neatly removed. Of course, doctor, you didn't work on the previous victim but it crossed my mind that that might be the reason for the removal of the genitals. A clever way to disguise it, if so. Do you think Ahmad might have had sex with his murderer?'

'Good point.' Flynn nods in agreement. 'I had wondered as much myself. I have searched for traces of semen but there are none to be found. None on the body, none on any of the clothing, including the underpants. Not to put too fine a point on it, when a young man of this kind of age is aroused sexually, minute seepages of semen sometimes leak from the penis. There was no sign of anything of that kind. But, I have still to do the internal exam so may find some other evidence inside.'

Tony looks as though he'd rather be anywhere in the world than here. But if he's going to stay in the force and make it as a DI one day, he's going to have to get used to pathologists, cadavers and the close-ups of violent deaths.

'On that, can you hold off until you have the go-ahead please, Edward. Apparently, the mother rang the station and is already fretting about the post-mortem on religious grounds. Shariah law, as you know, insists the body should be buried as soon as possible from the time of death.'

I am aware that this usually means that funeral planning and preparations begin immediately. There is a ritual washing of the body to be done before the body is wrapped in a special shroud and put on a bier to be buried.

I added, 'I am going to see her after I leave here to try to talk her round. I'll call you the moment I have something positive. If it's a no-go we'll have to let the coroner know. We're on delicate ground here, which I am sure you've come across before.'

'I have indeed. In this case, it would be a real shame if I am not permitted to do a full and comprehensive autopsy, so vital to discovering a possible reason outside of the randomness of this killing. I know religion has to be respected, but could we try begging special circumstances...?'

'I'll try as hard as I can, Edward, when I see the mother.'

'If it isn't one thing, it's a mother,' says Flynn.

I laugh.

'That's good.'

'It's Freud.'

'He'll do.'

'I have heard you have a reputation as one of the best detectives in the South London Met and are renowned for your toughness, effectiveness and dedication, inspector. And now, having met you I reckon you'd give most men more than a run for their money in terms of ability and strength of purpose.'

I am quite surprised by the doctor. Flattered, I suppose, but I feel his platitudes are unnecessary. He seems to think of us as a team, which I don't. His role is quite different to mine. But I say, 'You also have a good name. I have heard how painstaking and careful you are with your autopsies.'

'Well, you know, once you come to understand the beauty of the workings of the human form it becomes a fascination that takes you over. This is my calling, inspector. Apologies, I mean Jo.'

I reply, 'The official police line is that this murder confirms our suspicions of a racist motive. We are working on the idea that because castration is the ultimate terror of males, it follows that the killings and castrations are leaving a message to men of Asian, Caribbean, Black African or other ethnic races of colour to be afraid for their manhood and their lives.'

'I appreciate that you have to start the search somewhere for what is looking either like the hate crimes of some twisted killer's mind, or something altogether much harder to categorise,' says Flynn. He agrees the two could be racist crimes. 'You have all my sympathy. It is sickening to imagine the emasculations could be intended as a message to other men or ethnic minorities. I wish I could have found something more evidential to help you, but I have been over this young man more than once and through the scrapings of the fibres on the clothes and for the moment I am none the wiser. I'll keep looking. Perhaps something will show up. Good luck with the mother.'

I thank him, motion a relieved-looking Tony to follow and turn to leave.

That evening I go for two White Russians with Baileys and God, do I need them.

CHAPTER NINE

DI JO POLLITT

I stand in front of the whiteboard in Southwark Police Station where I pin close-up photos of Ahmad's face and neck and his mutilated body next to the photos of Winston Clarke.

Picking up a wooden pointer, I turn to face the room and clear my throat at full volume. Everyone stops what they are doing and looks up at me. Even though I say it myself, I am respected by my officers. 'Right. Your full attention, please.'

I point to the various photos and tell them we now have what is looking like a serial killer at large. I direct the long pointer at various pictures showing and explaining that both men suffered from asphyxiation by strangulation that was carried out by a garrotte-style cord knotted in the middle around the neck.

While I have to mention it in words, I don't go so far as to point to the wounds where both have also had their genitals removed as no one if they tried could possibly avoid noticing such graphic images.

The men in the room glance at one another, some pulling agonised expressions as they shuffle uncomfortably in their seats.

I tell them I do not want, I stress, do not want information regarding the mutilation of this second young man to get out. That we are determined to keep this out of the press. It will only cause unnecessary panic among the public and if this is a serial killer, which is likely, it could feed his twisted ego to read about it in the papers. So, I tell them, 'We keep this to ourselves, yes?'

Some murmur consent, others nod.

I inform them that to ensure no vital clues are overlooked, we're using the HOLMES computer programme. All police forces have access to it and can enter details of all serious crimes. HOLMES then processes the information discovered.

Explaining that teams of detective inspectors in charge of three or four detective constables will be assigned to the case to work under my direction, I tell them that I shall appoint those teams later today.

'But first I want to acquaint you with the latest details. Right. So: both men walking homeward from night work shifts. The choice of murder scenes in both cases may only be significant in as much as they were the quietest, least well-lit places on both men's homeward routes. This implies that both men were followed, perhaps from their places of work. We don't know, but for now we shall work on this assumption.'

'Both men were of different ethnic backgrounds so there is a possible racist motive here. In fact, Superintendent Green believes this to be a good likelihood. I want a list drawn up of all known far-right racist extremists who have a record of violence toward those groups. Our man could be among them.'

By midday, a determined young journalist has found and interviewed some friends of the Hussain family who learn through Ahmad's brothers about the castration and the news hits the London evening newspaper.

Men muffled in scarves and wearing flat caps rock on and stamp their feet trying to keep from freezing outside Tube stations and railway stations in the bitter cold. They stand next to bulletin boards with plastered messages reading:

SERIAL KILLER ON LOOSE IN LONDON

They wave copies of the paper and sell them in droves. Whatever the police try, it seems we are unable to keep people from knowing.

YOUNG LONDONER MURDERED AND CASTRATED

A twenty-four-year-old Pakistani, Ahmad Hussain, has been found murdered in a churchyard in the south London district of Tooting.

In a remarkably similar manner to the murder of Winston Clarke, the bus driver who was found dead in July on a street in Lambeth with his genitals removed, Ahmad Hussain was found garrotted with his genitals missing. Metropolitan Police detectives investigating the murder are appealing to the public for information on the attack which took place in the early hours of Thursday morning.

Officers were called to the grounds of the churchyard where amongst the gravestones they found Hussain dead from strangulation. A murder investigation has been launched and no arrests have been made so far. A post-mortem examination will be carried out at St Thomas' Hospital mortuary.

Leading the investigation, Detective Inspector Jo Pollitt, said: 'This was a sickening attack that has cruelly ended a young man's life. If anyone saw anything but has not yet come forward, please get in touch as soon as possible.'

It is now looking as though we do have a serial killer on our hands. Again, the murder has been committed in a quiet spot in the small hours with no witnesses. Both murders are within five miles of one another and in the same borough.

Where can I start? The super is on everyone's back at the station. It's his job, I suppose. But he's tough and he seldom hands out congratulations. Rarely, in all the time I have worked under him. Old school, more of a believer in punishment than in praise. One of these days, I am going to say something. He has become so certain these crimes are racially motivated. 'First a Black then a Pak – what else could it be?' is his indelicate way of putting it.

Having been educated in a mixed-race school and having friends and neighbours from various ethnic minorities, I so dislike the endemic racism within the Met and while I say nothing to my superior, I do raise my eyebrows in a manner that shows my disapproval.

Not that Green cares. He is Jewish himself and has felt the wrong end of many insults in his time. He knows all about the degrading language reserved for ethnic minorities and was being ironic when he said that. For all their bigotry, the police get it back in spades by being called 'pigs', 'filth', 'rozzers' and other worse nicknames on the streets.

In truth, Maurie detests racism deeply. He hangs his case on the fact that the BNP and other far-right parties are highly prominent in London at present and their followers hate the Blacks, Jews and the Asians. They have a lot of supporters and they attract a lot of neo-Nazi crazies. They are prevalent in Bermondsey, south of the river and not far from either crime scene.

He calls me to come to his office.

'Right away, Maurie.' I replace the receiver.

While he may be my boss, he does need the occasional reminder that it was not that long ago we worked side by side as detectives on an equal footing, and that I know him as well as anyone in the force.

I also know he doesn't really mean to sound as short as he sometimes does and under his recently acquired grumpy manner and antiquated, too-tight suits, the thickly-moustachioed man has a good soul.

A fine detective and once a genial character with whom you could share a joke, as he has aged and been given the job of 'super', he has become what I think of as a perfect example of the saying, 'it's lonely at the top'.

Sometimes, probably because of a slight facial similarity to Field Marshal Montgomery and his old-fashioned manner, he reminds me of a beleaguered general fighting a war.

Regarding this case, he insists I pursue the racist/fascist line and reluctant as I feel, I know it is the only thread we have to follow. I dread the world I'm about to delve into, having seen it before in all its particular nastiness. A world that contains some of the most narrow-minded, stupid and evil human beings I have ever come across.

CHAPTER TEN

MR AND MRS MAURICE GREEN

Maurice Green is at home savouring the dish of salted roast duck with cherry sauce, roast potatoes and sprouting broccoli, garnished with watercress that Marjorie has served for dinner that evening.

He is on his third glass of a Californian medium-bodied fruity Pinot Noir that he has decided is just the thing to accompany it. Beginning to feel a little heady, he cajoles his wife, 'Quite delicious. Well done, Marjorie. That was a very good sauce. And for afters?'

'Oh, Maurie! You jolly well wait and see. Enjoy what's in front of you and look forward to a nice surprise. But I will tell you this much: it's one of your favourites.'

He rolls his eyes in delight and chuckles. 'You do know how to keep your man happy, that's for sure, Mrs Green. Any chance of a hint?'

'No, definitely not, Mr Green. You'll have to wait and see.'

He loves his desserts as much as, if not a little more than, he loves his mains.

His wife knows her husband well and it is undeniable that

he gets a little extra frisson of pleasure from being unaware of what is to come.

She also knows that after dinner, Maurie will be in the best of moods to choose from the catalogue of West Indies holidays they have so often talked about but never settled upon choosing for his retirement next year. She cannot wait; it is so exciting. She will need to buy a whole new wardrobe... colourful holiday wear.

Marjorie imagines herself floating across a white sandy beach, nut brown from the sun, wearing a striking, large straw floppy hat, dark shades, a sexy black swimsuit, a floaty, pink diaphanous sarong wrapped around her waist that perfectly matches painted pink toenails on little tanned feet.

She sees the sand between those toes as she saunters casually towards a wooden sunbed strategically placed beneath a palm tree that inclines towards a calm turquoise sea where she will stretch out, fruity cocktail in one hand, thriller in the other to look up from her book occasionally to gaze out at the shimmering sunshine haze on the horizon.

In those moments she will be able to tell herself that all those days of tolerating Maurie's changeable moods, increasing self-concern and apparent inability to care about her needs have been worth putting up with...

CHAPTER ELEVEN

DI JO POLLITT

Cilla cycles over to spend the evening with me, which cheers me up. I have been feeling pretty low since the second murder. The realisation that we have a serial killer on our hands is not a happy one and that he is a highly clever fucker who leaves no trace of himself makes it worse. Ahmad was so young and it all feels so dreadfully sad. All because some cracked psycho has a crazy notion to go and take a life away in such a callous, apparently reasonless manner. How the hell are we ever going to catch him?

London seems an indomitably enormous place this evening and I am tired and dreading the task of tackling the far-right thugs that Maurie has foisted on me. I personally have my doubts. The murders seem far too clean for the likes of them. I'm fairly certain thugs would have made much more mess and used far more violence than has been employed in the two murders so far. I'm going to need a drink or four tonight.

Although I didn't plan to talk about them at home, Cilla takes a great interest in the murders and is determined to hear all the details. I suppose for her, it is like one of her detective thrillers.

We drink Baileys White Russians and discuss the murders at length and she agrees with me that they're unlikely to be racist and more likely the work of a homosexual serial killer.

We talk and talk and have more cocktails and get quite drunk and end up crashing on the sofa together which is unintended.

I wake up cold with my head on her lap at 3.15am and crawl upstairs to bed, having first covered my snoring friend with a duvet.

TUESDAY JANUARY 9TH, 1996

CHAPTER TWELVE

DI JO POLLITT

Twenty-five-year-old Colin Boyd has been in prison before for leading his gang of thugs to attack young blacks and Asians on the streets. The gang was a group of marauding far-right trouble-makers who went out looking for fights with ethnic minorities.

Colin lives in a run-down, grey apartment building in Bermondsey between London Bridge and a short walk from the south bank of the Thames. The neighbourhood is widely known as racist, insular and hostile to outsiders. It has a long-standing association with the British National Party, which stages marches through the district on St George's Day.

Although he lives alone, Colin is a dangerous customer and I'm not going to take any chances. When I pay him an unexpected visit on the Tuesday morning, I have decided not to inflame the situation by taking Tony, so instead bring a white-skinned detective sergeant and a uniformed police constable with me. I am astonished by the change in the man who answers the door.

The last time I saw Colin was before he was banged up

about three years ago. Now, a large swastika is tattooed across his forehead. He has also put on a vast amount of weight which emphasises the Neanderthal look about him.

Small, sunken, venomous eyes peer at me from beneath glowering, bushy eyebrows. A too large nose and a sulky downturned mouth with a full lower lip and lack of chin complete the picture. He must live on McDonald's takeaways. This gross-looking man is dressed in camouflage clothing. I want to say, *Love the outfit – you'd never be spotted in Bermondsey, roly-poly*. But instead, 'Hi, Colin. Remember me? DI Pollitt, Southwark Police. Just wondered if I could have a word with you down at the station?'

'What chew want round 'ere? I got nuffin' to say to pigs.'

'We'd just like to ask you a few questions, if that's all right?'

'Well, it's not. So you can jes' fuck off.'

'Put it like that, Colin, I'm afraid we shall have to formally insist you accompany us, but it would be so much nicer if we could all go quietly, wouldn't it?'

'I done nuffin' wrong. So why the fuck should I?'

'Just to help us with our enquiries, Colin.'

'What abaht?'

'About a couple of murders.'

'I ain't murdered no one. So who's been done then?'

'Let's talk about that back at the station, shall we, Colin?'

I nod at the constable who puts a hand on Colin's arm to guide him out of the flat but Colin spits a full mouthful at him and tries to slam the door on us. The DS has already got his foot in the door so with the PC's help, forces it open and a full fist fight takes place in the small hallway. Obscenities fly, forceful struggling takes place plus much spitting and attempted biting from the brutish young slob before, with some difficulty, the two policemen overcome him and cuff his hands behind his back.

As they fast-walk him to the waiting police car, I walk along beside them gabbling the obligatory, 'Colin Boyd, I am arresting you for the assault of two police officers in the execution of their duty...'

He yells and swears, 'Who's been done, then? I wanna know what you fuckin' lot's accusin' me of. You gotta say, you fuckin' pigs. You gotta fuckin' tell me.' He is bundled into the back of the police car between the two men. He keeps up the swearing, spitting, wriggling and shouting all the way back to the station.

But I am not going to tell him until much later. The idiot has played right into my hands. This means that he will spend time in a cell at the station while I have time to get a warrant and return with a forensic team to search his flat uninterrupted.

Back at Southwark, Colin is locked unceremoniously in a cell where the enraged man continues to shout and swear for a time but eventually shuts up and sits down on the bunk bed. Once quiet, he is taken some food and water.

Meantime, I apply for the warrant to search and get it within a few hours. I take a couple of forensic police guys with me to his flat.

Inside his home, it was clear that Boyd has been getting worse. He is now a member of a far-right group called Resist, a part of the British for Britain Party. Resist is supposed to protect the party and is famous for making threats against immigrants. He is reading neo-Nazi propaganda about an imminent race war. He has bought knives, swastika flags, knuckle-dusters, batons and a stun gun. He is researching bomb-making methods. He has written notes addressed to:

Nigers Jews Muslems
Get ready to meet youre end. Its gone to hurt

He seems intent on attacking everyone who isn't white and is clearly planning some catastrophic terror attack.

Yet another young nutter who's lost their way and who looks like they will end up in prison for most of their life. What a shame. What a waste.

We comb the place for any evidence relating to the two murders but can find nothing at all. But we find plenty of other stuff. Discouraged, I shall have to rely on the interview. But when I return to the station, I discover that the alibi Colin has given for the date of Ahmad's murder has been verified as cast-iron.

The man has been on a weekend away to visit another member of Resist in Harlow, Essex. Liverpool Street station has confirmed the sale of his return train ticket, paid for by credit card which checks out on his card statement. It doesn't go anywhere to help solving the murders but at least we have enough from the contents of his home to be able to bang up the nasty piece of work in Wandsworth Prison for some time.

Not long afterwards, the bastard that killed my mother is sentenced. He's going to the same jail where Colin will end up. I fantasise about them attacking and killing each other in there. The least they both deserve.

Witnesses said the man grabbed the young woman by her hair and was slapping her around the head when Mum, who was simply out shopping, went up to try to stop him. He turned on her and struck her a number of such vicious blows across the face and head that she fell to the pavement, where he then delivered some brutal kicks to her head and stomach. She never regained consciousness and died thirty-one hours later in hospital where they had fought to save her life.

My kind, loving, caring mum who never hurt a soul died trying to help another. How can it have happened?

At last the trial is over, and that effing bastard who after he had done with Mum then strangled his girlfriend who had been screaming at him to stop. He has been sent to jail for an indeterminate sentence.

TUESDAY MARCH 12TH TO MONDAY APRIL 1ST, 1996

CHAPTER THIRTEEN

DI JO POLLITT

Downcast, I have just returned to the station from visiting a rape victim in hospital who has been seriously hurt and terrified out of her wits. God, the woman was beaten so badly she can barely see out of either eye, her face is a pulp, her body a mass of bruises and cuts. She has a broken arm, bite marks everywhere and her injuries are among the worst I have ever seen.

Rapes are my most dreaded cases. When I see what some men are capable of doing to women, I find it intensely hard to contain my anger. At least in this case we've got the fucker. He's in the cells now.

The search for other far-right possible suspects in the garrotte cases continues. But we have no luck. The killer has left no trail and no evidence to work on. Soon even the press are going to tire of writing and talking about it.

The next day, the dreadful massacre at Dunblane in Scotland occurs. One morning a madman finds his way into the gymnasium of a primary school and shoots sixteen schoolchildren, a teacher and himself. This tragic event takes over the headlines and dominates the news for some time.

Matters concerning the London killer go quiet until the end of that month. I struggle with intermittent waves of grief at this time. I just cannot seem to get over or used to Mum's death. I probably need counselling, but when do I have the luxury of the time? Anyway, when I had the police therapist when a member of the public got shot (not killed, thank God) during a drug raid I led a couple of years ago, I found it no help at all.

CHAPTER FOURTEEN

JIM HAYDEN

Drivers is a family business going back fifty-nine years. It supplies all kinds of fruits, vegetables, salads and herbs from the run-of-the-mill to the exotic to retailers and producers within the famous Borough Market in the district of Southwark and around the city of London. They deliver fresh produce daily and are open to the public during the night as a wholesale stand. At night a few workers package the produce ready for delivery the next morning.

One such packer is young Jim Hayden who lives in Bermondsey with his parents and his little sister. His shift ends at 5.30am on Thursday March 28th. He gets his week's pay package from the guvnor tomorrow and then on Saturday he is real excited about the football. Dad's got tickets to see the Lions playing at The Den that afternoon.

Millwall are sliding down the league tables toward the second division this season and are playing for their lives trying to crawl their way back up. Saturday is an important match against Crystal Palace and the Lions are playing at home. They have every chance.

Like his docker dad and grandad before him, Jim has always

been a Millwall fan. He and his dad will be there cheerin' 'em on and chantin' with the Bushwacker fans everyone's scared of.

But you's okay if you's on their side and like them, you's singin', 'No one likes us, we don't care.' He can already picture himself wearing his blue-and-white barred scarf, his baker boy flat cap and his navy hoodie with the pic of the white fighting lion in a white circle on the front as he roars along with the crowd.

Jim makes his way through the streets and alleys that he has grown up with and he'll soon be home to grab some nosh and shut-eye. Then only one more day before it'll be Saturday.

He and Dad'll get to the stadium in plenty of time before things kick off, and he doesn't mean the match; he means trouble, as it always does there. The Den is near where they live so that's easy.

Half skipping down an alleyway, he sees the early light of dawn is already creeping up to illuminate his way. For some reason, perhaps a dark cloud crosses his sky, Jim feels an unexpected chill when someone speaks to him from behind. He stops and turns.

What an odd sight. *What the fuck?* he thinks and almost doesn't answer. But then he does and for some reason he hesitates and makes to pick up the dropped piece of paper.

If the eager young man had lived to see the match, he would have been heartbroken that the Lions lost 1–4. But that morning at just 5.46am, at the age of twenty-one years old, Jim Hayden breathed his last breath.

CHAPTER FIFTEEN

It had been two months and I'd been itching to get out again. But I had to be sure conditions were right. I had left it late and had had no luck and was about to give up for the night when I saw the young one. Just luck.

There he was. A spring in his step. A slight lad, skinny. Ginger hair cut very short. A bit taller than I'd taken on before but on account of how spindly he was, I knew I wasn't out of my depth.

As I followed and got closer, I felt the creeping elation, and adrenaline surged through my body. An incredible sensation. My heart thumped as I spoke softly to him and just as I wanted, he stopped.

A slip of a person, must have been a late developer. He was a little aggressive and almost didn't pick up the paper but when he saw the pleading look in my eyes, changed his mind and did so. Reminded me of how Mamma always gave in to me when I looked at her in a special way, particularly after that awful father of mine had departed.

He puffed his last breath onto my cheek before he fell into line, stooped and never made it upright again. Nipped behind, cord over the head and round the neck. Knee up, pushed forward, jerked back hard as I could.

Oh, but it felt as good as the others, maybe better because I have got to know the ropes. I like the pun. I could take my time with him and I wasn't rushed. I felt his body close against mine, struggling and twitching for all its worth. I feel both good and bad when this happens.

Why am I doing this?

My heart raced but I was so in control. Once he was down and gone, I looked at him for a little while.

Pulled his jeans down. Surprisingly well-hung for such a lean one. I did the cut with particular care. The ecstasy was strong when I carefully dropped the bits into the jar inside the bag, waved him goodbye and headed back. I had to walk fast through the streets that were growing lighter by the minute. I have saved many from what that boy might have done with that apparatus of his.

I wanted to run but the few people around might have noticed. Another lesson learned. It was nearly 6.30 by the time I got home. Mustn't leave it so late next time.

CHAPTER SIXTEEN

DI JO POLLITT

A large herd of grey horses, ears back, teeth bared, are galloping flat out toward me, leaving me nowhere to run but into the sea behind me. I am going to have to swim for my life. A sudden bell rings to remind me that I cannot swim. It sounds again.

I wake with a jolt. I roll over, rub my eyes, knock a black cat off my legs and disturb a ginger on the pillow next to me. The animals yawn, stretch and reposition themselves. Through slit eyes they watch me while I fumble to turn on the bedside light switch. I have to squint through half-closed eyes to read the alarm clock, the light hurting my eyes. Twenty-three minutes past six o'clock in the morning. I usually rise at 7.15am. I grapple with the mobile, clear my throat, always croaky first thing in the morning.

'Hello... yes... right... yes, okay... Can you just let me write that down, I mean... Sorry, could you just repeat that...'

Now waking properly, I sit myself up, swing legs out of bed and grab the open notepad and biro kept by the bed just for this purpose. Scribbling down an address on the top page, I say, 'Okay,' and listen with attention as more details are given. I jot them down in my own kind of shorthand. 'Got it... Sounds grim. Right you are... quick as I can. Yes. Thanks. See you later.'

———————

Later that day, I stand with Dr Flynn in the mortuary looking at the cadaver of the red-haired young man.

The pathologist is able to offer no more evidence than he has on the previous murder. He seems dejected as well as aggravated and says he feels almost guilty that he has so little to say but that this murderer is extremely intelligent and is going to take a lot of catching.

As eager as he knows I am to find the brute, Edward feels my reputation is not being helped by his inability to trace any forensic clues on the bodies left by this killer. As with the two previous corpses, there is a large, livid circular bruise in the lower centre of the back. Holding a magnifying glass over it he studies it for some time before measuring it with a minutely precise tool. Reading the measurements out loud, he says it has to be the knee in the back again. Disconsolate, I return to the station none the wiser.

CHAPTER SEVENTEEN

DCS MAURICE GREEN

Will the keeper ever be caught?

Third victim of gruesome murder

When will the horror end?

Police Fail to stop serial killer

Garrotted and castrated!

Macabre and shocking says Police Chief

A third victim is up on the whiteboard. Another young man. Although the three victims have been under the age of forty, there is no telling what the killer might do next. They all dread the thought of another murder but know it is likely.

Because they have decided he keeps the genitals as trophies, one of the tabloids has nicknamed the murderer 'The Keeper', a bland tag that so belittles the awfulness of his crimes that it almost makes light of them... and it has caught on with the public.

Maurice Green sits at his desk in his office. Hoping he will look deep in thought about some greatly important police matter, he tilts his head back, swivels his chair away from the office, closes his eyes and wonders what Mrs Green is serving this evening. Didn't she mention something about steak Bordelaise? If so, he trusts she'll have kept the remains of the bottle she'd used to make the sauce – a fine Bordeaux which he could drink with it... he'll have to wait and see what she's cooked up. Nowadays they have replaced supper with dinner.

While Marjorie might not be the most exciting companion in many ways, what a cook she has turned out to be. She watches all the cookery programmes on TV and buys all the latest cookery books. Since she's retired from nursing, she's been on a fine dining cookery course where she's learned a great deal. Recipe books and cooking pans make for easy birthday and Christmas presents and she never fails to come up with delicious three-course dinners. That is the joy of living with Marjorie.

She might have deviated from Bordelaise and done something entirely different. It could be fish, there really is no telling.

Last night they had a starter of watercress soup with home-made parmesan biscuits, then a rack of lamb with a mint and balsamic vinegar crust, mashed potato, Savoy cabbage and glazed carrots followed by a dessert of lemon and ginger cheesecake, one of Maurie's favourites. He washed it down with a bloody marvellous French Merlot and his mind savours the memory for a few moments before it turns to wondering what she has in store for tonight.

He exhales then wrenches his mind away and pivots himself back to business.

Gazing across the piles of paperwork in front of him through the plain glass window to the rest of the office where he can keep an eye on most of the desks, Maurice Green watches Jo Pollitt at hers. He feels a sudden pang of intense guilt. He knows she is no nearer to knowing where to start to look for the bloody killer than she was after the first murder. The brute was out there not only destroying the lives of young men but causing huge grief to their families, loved ones and friends.

How the super wishes he could take Jo's place. If he was still a working detective instead of a superintendent... Trapped behind a desk was not his dream of joining the police, nor had it been his idea of being a senior detective. He shouldn't be dreaming about what was for dinner tonight. He should be out there catching the bastard.

A naturally active man who operates best at ground level and finds this job frustrating (although he and Marjorie do not object to the very decent salary) he is dreading retirement a lot less these days.

In fact, there are times he would positively prefer to be on the golf course or walking the dog than sitting here in his office having to deal with too much stuff. The administration work is never-ending and his state of mind is not helped by the current worry. He just wants to reach his retirement in thirteen months without too much stress – not too much to ask, surely?

Stretched to its limits, the Metropolitan CID has already lost numbers of detectives who have been caught in corruption plot scandals and morale is low within the department.

When the next murder might be, he has no idea but Maurice Green cannot help hoping the killer will wait till after his retirement.

CHAPTER EIGHTEEN

DI JO POLLITT

I am going through paperwork in the office and finding it hard to concentrate. The case niggles at my brain, asking again and again what I can do to find a suspect, let alone a culprit. I have decided the best way to tackle the super is not to tell him I have received a call from a man called Patrick Delaney. A well-known criminal profiler who had had much success in recent years with helping the police find murderers, he has called me saying he would love to be involved as he already has some ideas about the killer.

The problem is, I've known the super well for a long time. He doesn't stand for any of what he calls psycho-babble and maintains an ingrained cynicism when it comes to the psychology profession. The best and only way with the man is to let him think that the idea of employing such a person is his own. I shall have to tread extremely carefully with the subject.

The superintendent glances through the glass to see me waving at him and beckons me to join him. He has a particularly despondent look about him following the third murder. I approach his office slowly, rehearsing what to say before I knock on his door. I must choose my words wisely.

In his office, he gestures for me to sit down. His state of mind is not helped by the fact that recently his back has started to ache. He shuffles uncomfortably in his chair. Firstly, I sympathise with him over his painful condition and offer to run to the pharmacist to get him some painkillers. Buttering-up tactics.

He is grateful, as I am the only one in the office who has dared to show him pity. He explains he is already on some pills given by the doctor and I can tell he enjoyed my solicitous offer. He even manages a smile.

'What can I do for you, Jo?'

'Oh sir,' *plenty of sirs must follow* 'I'm getting nowhere with this effing killer, sir. May I ask you, please...' *Let him think he's the brain-power.* I pause. 'Am I missing something? I mean, what might I have overlooked? I have racked my brains and cannot think what else to try. Do you have any suggestions, sir?'

He is relieved I haven't referred to the man by the name that even he occasionally slips up and uses, 'The Keeper', the press-invented name that reminds frightened Londoners what he does and that greatly irritates the superintendent as he feels, like we all do, that it somehow softens the horror of the crimes.

Avoiding the word *psychological* that will definitely rile him, I bring up the subject of offender profilers and, knowing full well how he will react, ask what he thinks about them.

He makes it quite plain that he is certain any correct results are luck. In his opinion, this new craze is a waste of time and he's convinced there's no substitute for good old slogging detective work. I casually mention that this man called Patrick Delaney has rung and offered his services and then that he has been highly successful in helping capture a number of killers in the past few years.

I slip a few stapled pages of A4 in a plastic folder under Maurie's nose. They are a profile of Patrick Delaney's eleven years' work helping the Met. 'Have a look at that later would you, sir?'

We avoid the subject of profilers now and I leave our short meeting with no more to go on.

As I am leaving his office, as though I'd just thought of it, I murmur in a kind of offhand way, 'Buy you a pint at the Queen's Head at the end of the day, sir?'

Knowing he can never resist a free lager he jumps at the offer. That is when I have him. As the other detectives are well aware, after a pint the super is always more amenable, especially in the evenings when he's thinking about filling his ever-expanding belly with Mrs Green's cooking. Having been extra careful with the 'sirs' today, before I close his door I say, 'Oh that's great. I'll really look forward to seeing you later, sir. 6.30 okay for you?'

'Just right. Only the one pint, mind. Mrs Green won't be a happy puppy if I'm late home for dinner.'

Actually, it's you who won't be a happy puppy if you're late home for it. 'Of course not, sir.'

CHAPTER NINETEEN

DCS MAURICE GREEN

Maurice watches Jo Pollitt leave his office and wend her way back to her desk.

He knows Jo better than she thinks he does. He knows that she is going to have another go later at persuading him to employ Delaney.

He also knows he is going to accept her inducement. The pressure is growing daily. Whatever he thinks about these jumped-up psycho-babble profile people, results are desperately needed. He knows he is going to have to try everything. Whatever the police do to try to prevent the press finding out about the castrations, the buggers always find a way. The force is ultimately answerable to the Home Office and now even the Home Secretary is starting to ask questions.

The stress is getting to him. Superintendent Green is a human being, not a machine that can produce a guilty killer at the press of a button. This particular one was an extremely clever bastard who left no trace of himself.

They have no idea where he comes from and no previous criminal on police records appears to be the man they are after.

The killer is a well-hidden needle in the giant haystack of south London's crowded streets.

Maurice likes Jo and knows just how good a detective she is. In fact, he has always had something of a soft spot for her.

Pollitt has a strong, good-looking face with humour lines around the lips and large, intelligent green eyes that exude confidence. Her unruly thatch of dark wavy hair that will never stay where she wants it adds a touch of charm that draws others as much as Green to her. She dresses carelessly and seemingly not to attract, but her clothes, either baggy trouser suits or loose jackets and trousers, cannot hide her tall, just short of graceful figure. She has a good bosom, Maurie noted a long time ago. Just right as far as he is concerned. Neither too big nor too small but just right.

Maurice never worries that when she sometimes feels his eyes peering at her across the station she might think it was for any other reason than he is desperate for her to pull in results. He has often wondered why she has no partner or husband but has never been brave enough to ask. She's a strong, spirited woman who would need a powerful man to take her on, that would be certain. He wonders whether if he'd been younger...

The superintendent understands Jo's reasons for wanting to bring in help as these murders are as mysterious as they are unusual. That the murderer is mentally ill is not in question.

Until the young man from Bermondsey was murdered, Maurice's gut told him that the murders were likely to be the work of some crazy racist individual or group, but this latest lad was as British as the Union Jack. So they are further up a gum tree than ever with no idea where to start or where to look.

There are many other ongoing cases of greater importance that need results more than finding this murderer. The department has just succeeded in cracking a large drugs operation run by London gangsters so the press should be extolling his force but this bloody Keeper has got the attention of the journalists and the public, who love nothing so much as a gruesome killer.

Once they can put this one to bed, they will be able to divert the force back to preventing the spread of crack cocaine that is growing faster than they can believe. It is only March but this year in his district there have already been nine murders, twenty-one attempted murders and twenty-three other shootings related to drug gangs embroiled in turf wars over crack.

Maurie scans the document about Patrick Delaney in preparation for when he sees Jo later. He won't tell Jo but it makes for some pretty impressive reading.

By the time he leaves the pub later this evening, the chief superintendent has gone against everything he believes in and agreed to get Patrick Delaney in on the case. He has promised Jo he will call the man first thing the following morning.

'I'll buzz you once I've spoken to this Delaney character.'

'Oh Maurie, I can't thank you enough.'

'Sir.' He smiles half-heartedly

'Sir.' Jo grins widely back.

They leave the pub together and as she turns left towards her Golf and he strolls the other way to his Jaguar, she doesn't see Maurice glance over his shoulder at her retreating figure.

Nor is she privy to his thoughts of how unwittingly attractive the woman is, nor that for him this could not be a more satisfactory result. Whichever way it falls, he will still come out on top. If this Delaney character fails, which in Maurice's heart of hearts he believes he will, the super will be able to say he had never thought it a good idea but had had his arm twisted.

But if the profiler helps them catch the murderer then Maurice can say he did the right thing by calling him in on the case. A win-win, he thinks as he calls Mrs Green from his mobile phone to let her know he's on his way back after a busy one, and to ask casually, by the way what was it she had said was for dinner tonight?

'We're starting with goat's cheese and red onion tarte tatin – I know you like them – and for the main course it's...'

Bordelaise? He crosses his fingers. He's been salivating at the thought all day.

'...Entrecôte Bordelaise accompanied with frites potatoes and spinach a la crème.'

She's even doing it with frites. And he is very partial to spinach, particularly the way she does it with a little cream in it. Oh, he could kiss her. He will when he gets home. That deep-fat fryer he'd bought her for her birthday really has paid dividends.

CHAPTER TWENTY

DI JO POLLITT

My extension phone buzzes. I pick up to hear the voice that is today considerably sharper and snappier than it has been the previous evening. He almost barks at me.

Green's mood has changed again. Evidently smarting from having just agreed to spend some of his precious budget on employing a criminal profiler even though only for a limited term, he snaps, 'Spoken to Delaney who will start this afternoon and is to report to me in my office at 2pm as I shall expect you to do, Inspector Pollitt. No time like the present. We'll go through the case with him then. You'd better have everything ready to show the man.'

'Of course, sir. Thank you so much, sir. I'm sure you won't regret it.'

'We shall see.' Sarcasm tinges his words. 'Fourteen hundred hours. Don't be late, Pollitt.'

He sounds irritated with me. I have persuaded him into doing this. Or have I? That is what he wants me to feel. Maurie's no fool and a tough old buzzard. I've seldom seen him give in when he's really made up his mind about something. The truth, I think, is that he wants to be able to blame me if it doesn't work out; and, conversely, take the praise for it himself if it does. Wiley old sod. He is, like I am, stuck with what to do next and has realised we have got to the point where we have to try just about everything. No *sir* this time.

Unusually for the way things are going lately, I actually slept well last night and feel pretty good today. The prospect of having someone to share the burden of finding whoever is doing these murders is a huge relief and I'm experiencing a renewed sense of hope.

At 1358, I sit silently in a chair in front of the super's desk as we wait for Delaney. Maurie ignores me and works at papers while I stare at the floor.

At exactly 1400, he knocks on the door. Before Maurie has finished saying, 'Come in', a pair of startlingly blue eyes behind a large pair of horn-rimmed spectacles coupled with a broad grin and a square dimpled chin has popped itself around the door.

A man of medium height with a dark-brown, shaggy, unstyled haircut and unshaven stubble who couldn't be more than in his mid-thirties, follows the face into the room, saunters over to the super's desk and before the surprised Maurie can speak, stretches out his hand and waits until the DCS falteringly stands up and extends his to be gripped and shaken firmly.

'Chief Superintendent Green,' he says, 'Patrick Delaney at your service.'

Having completely back-footed the super, he then turns to me. 'And you must be the highly-respected DI Pollitt?'

I place the Irish lilt to be from the Dublin area. I'm pretty good at accent locating.

Maurie motions to an armchair with an authoritative wave of his hand. 'Right. Sit down, Mr, um, Delaney.'

This cocky, unkempt young so-and-so is going to have to watch his P's and Q's if he is going to work for Chief Superintendent Green and he'd better find this out straight away.

Unworried, Delaney slowly removes his brown leather coat under which he is wearing a check shirt and faded denim jeans. A pair of well-worn caramel-coloured Timberland boots adorn his feet. Casually draping the coat over the mock leather armchair, he sits down, makes himself comfortable, balances one foot on the knee of the other leg and quietly studies the superintendent's face.

It seems a markedly cheeky thing to do. I wonder whether the self-assurance is bluster and due to nervousness, but the guy doesn't seem in the least uneasy.

Unused to such apparent disrespect, Maurie is clearly put out as he flaps a hand at me. 'Inspector Pollitt will fill you in.'

While I outline the three murders, Delaney keeps quiet and concentrates carefully. He jots notes in a scruffy little notebook he produces from his coat pocket. Now, maybe, we'll get somewhere.

The feeling grows stronger later when I take Delaney through to the incident room to study the whiteboards with the photographs and notes and what little evidence has been collected so far. During this time he still says little but scribbles away.

In spite of his super-self-confident entrance, he gives the impression of having a thoughtful mind. I hope his silences say more than most people's words. He appears to listen carefully and his eyes glisten with intelligence as he takes in not only what he is hearing but the manner and details of what is being said during the debriefing.

When we finish, I quietly mention that the super is somewhat old-fashioned and likes people working for him to be respectful. 'In an army sort of way, if you know what I mean.'

Delaney flashes a smile and says he knows exactly what I mean and that he'd seen it when they met earlier. I clear my throat and suggest in my most tactful tone that when he's next in the super's office it might be best not to sit with one leg balanced on the other particularly when wearing rugged outdoor walking boots as the old boy will take that sort of thing as a personal affront.

'Really? That bad?' says Delaney, removing his spectacles and rolling his eyes. He fixes me with a sky-blue gaze. 'Okay then. Point taken. Sorry I put my walking boot in it so quickly.'

Replacing the horn-rims, he smiles at the corner of his mouth and I giggle and we know we are going to get on.

'I'll tread more carefully next time.' We laugh some more. I begin to think that the man's self-assurance comes neither from vanity nor arrogance but from a calm belief in what he has been taught and has learned about the human psyche. After we have sat either side of my desk and then grabbed some lunch in the canteen, I decide I really like him and that we are going to work well together. He is adamant that he's not going to jump to any conclusions but rather that he wants to mull over all he has heard and seen and that he will talk to me the following day with any ideas he may have come up with.

At about 1730, he shakes my hand. 'It's been a very interesting afternoon, Detective Pollitt. I've enjoyed meeting you and think we're going to get along fine together. Quite a case, this one. These are strange killings. I've much to mull over. I know it's Saturday, but may I call you tomorrow morning?'

'Of course, I shall be working tomorrow though I'll take Sunday off unless anything happens to prevent it. I've enjoyed meeting you too. Let's kick-start our working relationship by dispensing with formalities. I'm Jo. Have you got far to go?'

'Camden Town, easy enough Tube journey on the Northern line. Bye Jo and as you know, I'm Patrick. I'll call you tomorrow.' He flashes another of those wide grins as he waves goodbye.

CHAPTER TWENTY-ONE

PATRICK DELANEY, CRIMINAL PROFILER

W hen I get home to my little flat in Camden, I go straight to my big old Victorian desk. A muddle of pens, papers, newspapers cuttings, photographs and hand-written A4 pages and notebooks are stacked precariously on its top. I push some aside to make room to write something and the stack threatens to topple and fall to the ground.

Somehow there is room for a half-eaten pizza that lies abandoned on a plate, a couple of empty lager bottles nearby and a black baseball cap with a white NY on it that has seen better days.

I sit down on my rickety old captain's swivel chair with the cracked, red leather seat. Scanning the muddle, I tell myself tomorrow I will go through it and sort it all out and that a lot can and must be chucked out. But I know I won't. I just never do seem to get around to it. The *now* is always so much more interesting.

I rock back in the chair and think about the day that has just gone. I like Jo Pollitt; she's sound and knows her stuff. We are going to get on fine, I felt her respect for me and know she will listen to me and that I will be able to persuade her toward my viewpoint when I feel the need. I wouldn't be able to work with her if not. I feel I'm in a good position and should be able to influence the outcome of this murder hunt. That stuffy old super could prove a bit of a stumbling block but... hopefully he won't be involved apart from our having to report to him from time to time.

I study the notes I made earlier. Then I lean forward and look at a piece of A4 on the desktop on which there is a large circle within which I have previously drawn three numbered X's and initials of the victims to represent the three murders. From the first murder on, I drew a rough depiction of the river Thames and added the names of the areas where the killings occurred on the London map. The Tube stations nearest to those places are marked as well. I plot where the next one should be. My pencil hovers over the map.

My stomach decides I should eat so I pick up last night's plate, take it into the kitchen, empty the pizza remains into the waste bin, put the dirty plate to be washed up later in the sink, open the freezer, find another pizza, stick that in the microwave and wait until it is cooked. Finding another plate in a disorganised cupboard and some cutlery in a drawer, I put the pizza on the plate and take the food back to the desk along with a couple of bottles of cold lager from the fridge.

Sucking the pencil top, thinking and scribbling, replenishing the lagers until there are four more bottles in the stand, I am at my desk until well past midnight. A new half-eaten pizza replaces the old (I don't actually like them much – they are just so convenient).

The next morning I call Pollitt to tell her I want to visit the crime scenes for myself and that I will come and see her on Monday if that will suit. She offers to drive me to the various locations but I politely refuse explaining I would prefer to travel by underground in order to take routes the killer may have taken.

CHAPTER TWENTY-TWO

DI JO POLLITT

Monday morning and Delaney and I are sitting side by side at a long table in the almost empty canteen at the police station. A cleaning lady is mopping the floor at the far end of the large room. We each have a coffee from the machine which does little to inspire creative thought patterns but it is quiet here and I can't be distracted by phones and people.

Delaney takes his well-thumbed little notebook from his inside coat pocket, opens it and scans his notes. 'There are some striking and highly unusual things about these murders. Firstly, there is no attempt made to hide or cover the victims, which are left for all to see on open streets. The murderer takes a great risk by killing in populated areas, albeit at night... one tiny mistake, i.e. someone comes along or the victim cries out and they could be caught. So, we can conclude from that that we have a person who doesn't mind, perhaps enjoys, taking risks. Then we must consider the method. Garrotting is a highly efficient, quick and relatively painless way to kill someone. Our man or woman...'

I look at him askance. '...Woman?'

'It can't be ruled out, Jo.'

'Bloody hell, man. How could a woman manage such murders?'

'There are plenty of strong women around, Jo, look in the mirror.'

'Oh, for heaven's sake!' I hesitate, then, 'Uh-oh – not a particularly good April fool, Patrick.'

Delaney is not smiling. 'I am serious. There are few female serial killers but they have existed and we cannot rule the possibility out at this stage. Open minds are essential.' He continues, 'Besides, you see, Jo, there's a dichotomy here that I can't quite get my head round. Garrotting is a typically efficient uninvolved male act of the disposal of another, whereas with the removal of the genitalia, an emotional involvement is definite and an almost female care is taken. Then there are the fibres left behind – but no other traces – a highly unusual crime scene... Perhaps a part of the murderer hopes to be caught? They make no effort to conceal the bodies where they might not be found so easily or quickly and they take tremendous risks killing on open streets even though it is dark and late.'

At this point, a couple of officers wearing stab-proofs enter the room and walk to a table well away from us where they seat themselves and crack open cans of Coke. Delaney lowers his voice. 'The whole case is so very strange,' he says. 'Also, it seems the victims are approached in each case as there are no obvious hiding places the killer could have waited behind to jump out from.'

'I believe you're right, but just think it's highly unlikely it's a woman.'

'But why castrations?' he asks. 'Why would a man want to castrate another? For a guy this would be a highly personal act of revenge on someone they knew. But for a killer who doesn't know the victims and takes the genitalia away with them? Of course, we cannot be certain they do not dispose of them elsewhere but why would they bother to do that? They must do it because they want to keep them. Why would a man want to keep them? A homosexual possibly, a female yes. But I think, because of the lack of hatred here, that if it's a homosexual he would feel too much empathy or even transference, if you like, with his victim to emasculate him... Oh, I don't know but I do know that we must keep open minds, Jo, open minds.' He flashes that blue-eyed grin.

'Okay then, I suppose...' I don't like it but I have to be gracious. 'So, you were saying?'

'That this killer is not violent. Another highly unusual thing. That they treat the victim with care. In a sense they treat them gently, kindly even.'

I almost interrupt again. I don't like where this is going. But I have to let him finish this time. Perhaps, after all it was a mistake to have employed him. Sure, I like the guy but it is beginning to sound as though he is simply spouting gobbledegook for which he is getting paid. I suck on a cigarette. 'Gently, kindly?'

'Yes. As gentle and as kind as it is possible for a murderer to be. Unlike most serial killers, this one is not choosing to inflict anger, rage or violence upon their victims. This one has killed quickly with as little pain as possible and done the damage after death. It is almost as though they don't want to hurt them. Another thing is the castrations appear to have been done cleanly and carefully as though showing respect to the victims. It is turning out to be a weird psychological profile. One thing for sure, our murderer is a highly intelligent person.'

'I would agree but what makes you say that?'

'In that, even though it is dark and there is no one around, that he or she can manipulate his or her victims into just about permitting him or her an easy chance to kill and by the fact that in all three cases he has left no trace of his or herself. That takes great cunning and intelligence.'

I think through what Delaney has said. Now, the more I think about it, after my initial over-reaction, I see that everything he says makes sense. Thank God after all, I back-pedal, that Maurie has agreed to allow him to help.

To catch someone is going to take a lot and this man can think way beyond the box. And if thinking beyond it can help me, then good. The murderer may be intelligent but so is Delaney. Everything he can tell me will help with what I have to do. And I need every little shred of help, from inside and outside every effing box there is.

Then he says, 'I have a suspicion that our killer may suffer from dissociative disorder as a result of some trauma that happened when he or she was a child. Parts of his or her personality may be angry and easily aroused. Because of the dissociation within the person, the anger is an emotion that is not integrated into the whole.'

He removes his glasses and twiddles them around in his fingers. This seems to be a habit of Delaney's that helps him think.

'So, though people with dissociative disorder are responsible for their behaviour just as others are, regardless of which part of them may be acting, they will feel very little control of these raging parts of themselves.'

I listen carefully to this clever man's diagnosis of the killer and hope it will help us somehow. I gaze out of the canteen window that overlooks the car pool as Delaney continues, 'The bizarre thing about this is that other dissociative parts of them may dodge and avoid anger as a reprehensible emotion. These divisive parts of a person may influence the whole person to avoid conflict with others, parts of themselves at any cost or to avoid setting healthy boundaries out of fear of someone else's disapproval or even rage. But there are occasions when the angry part must have its day.'

The sky is grey; it looks like rain is on the way.

'I suspect this may be the psychological profile we are chasing. But only suspect, mind you. It's just a guess. The reason I have arrived at this idea is because of the contradictory behaviour of the murderer.'

'In what sense?' I ask.

'Chop off the genitals – but so very neatly. Why? Why not hack them off? The method is at variance with the deed. Almost as though one part of him or her has a desire to de-sex and brutalise the victim yet another wants to do it with care and with as little mess as possible, as though they do not want to cause the victim any suffering. But this is crazy stuff because, of course, the victim is already dead.'

'It's crazy all right,' I mutter while he carries on.

'This conflicted attitude would also account for the method of killing. Quick and relatively painless. That is why I used the word "gently" to describe the murders.'

Now, I am properly impressed.

Delaney stops, puts his glasses back on and stares out of the window. 'The victims are getting younger,' he says. 'Have you noticed? I think the first was a try-out, if you know what I mean. I mean, I think it was our murderer's first attempt and age was less important then. The other two have been a decade younger.'

'True, they have. What do you think that means?'

'That young men are the flavour of the month, I suppose.'

I shudder and wish he could put it a bit more delicately. These are people he is talking about.

'Really, Patrick!'

'Sorry. Okay. So anyway, here so far are my initial thoughts.' He passes me his notebook. On two facing pages he has written out a list.

Colour: Probably White
Definitely Intelligent
Enjoys risk-taking
Method: Non-violent/Careful/gets close causing no alarm – how? Hides/pounces or approaches victims?
Reason: Anger? Desire? Why no attempt at intercourse?
Motive – Victim and trophies.
Impotent male or angry, man-hating female?
Gender: Male or female.
Times of death: Darkness: How does killer see? Torch? Check moons?
Victims: Chosen for gender, age, height, weight, then propitious appearance
Behaviour: Risk-taker – see locations. No attempt to hide bodies. Wants vics found?? Proud of manner of killing and removal of genitals. Secret Exhibitionist? Why Trophies or souvenirs? Deviant?
Type: Male/female? Married/single? Children? Sexual persuasion? Impotent? Poss rejected by father who left or withheld love. Trauma when young? Anger with men – why?
Ethnicity: Prob white. Stats: Asians don't usually kill Asians and Blacks don't usually kill Blacks and v.v.

I say, 'So you think he/she kills for the genitals rather than the thrill of killing? Surely not?'

Delaney leans back in his chair, takes off his spectacles again and once more twirls them in his hand. 'I think it's a bit of both, although I think the genitals are the ultimate prize, if you like.

But the definitive reason for the kill is the victim, the prey. That's what we need to concentrate on. Why does he choose them? I am certain they are not simply picked at random. They are all men under the age of forty and if you exclude Winston as "practice", the next two are under thirty and progressively younger.'

'So bizarre.'

'It is.'

We are silent for a while. Delaney puts his glasses back on, sucks his pen, removes his horn-rims, wipes them with a handkerchief and puts them on again. Then he studies his notes. I stare out of the window and around the room.

'Whoever they are, they are playing with us, Jo.'

'I know.'

'There will be more to come.'

'I know that too.'

'And the next will be younger still.'

I shudder.

SATURDAY MAY 18TH TO MONDAY MAY 20TH, 1996

CHAPTER TWENTY-THREE

ROBIN LEATHAM

It was a great gig. The Minstrel is such a cool venue. Rob Leatham is feeling very good indeed. A lot of their fans were there. The place was packed and the band had been tight and played really well. He'd been playing and singing his best too. His new songs went down really well. The crowd had loved 'For Real' and 'Wash-Out City'.

It had helped that beautiful Lexa had come and had hooted and danced and waved her long hair and arms and hips about and rocked to the music and looked so cool and just soooo sexy. Her being there had encouraged him to perform his best. They'd had two encores and girls in the audience had shouted, 'We love you, Rob.'

Then Lexa has come back with him to Oz's parents' place in Chelsea afterwards and they've done quite a lot of dope and a few lines and he and Lexa are now getting it on. He is pretty stoned by now and they've drunk quite a lot of Jack Daniels and just at the big moment when they're about to sneak into Oz's bedroom and do the deed, and they're so hot and he has a steaming great hard-on, Oz's dad suddenly comes into the room and causes a stink about them smoking and making a noise at

2.30 in the morning. He's all fired up. So uncool and he tells them all to leave.

So that stops the fun. Then Lexa calls a cab, which he and she share, to take her back to her parents' gaff in South Ken. At least they're able to carry on with the sex stuff in the back of the cab until she gets home but it isn't far so he drops her off there and takes the taxi on to Victoria so he can catch the Tube home.

He can't afford to take it all the way home. He's a bit broke at the moment. By the time the four of them split the money, he earns very little gigging with the band. But he occasionally does some gardening for some of his mother's well-off friends and he just about gets by and, all in all, life is pretty cool.

When Rob arrives at Clapham South station, he almost leaves his guitar behind but just remembers in time and seizes it before he stumbles out of the Tube onto the platform.

He turns left out of the exit onto the street and crosses Clapham Common, notorious as a place for gay cruising so he's ready with his polite but firm no thanks in case he's approached. Occasionally, he glances over his shoulder to be sure he isn't being followed until he reaches another road that he crosses again, then winds through a few more streets towards his home where his mother and his younger brother are asleep.

Still glowing with the buzz of the evening, he can't wait to get it on with Lexa again and finish the business properly next time.

He turns onto the street where he lives and remembers to be sure not to wake his mum as she gets in such a grump if her nights are disturbed and he becomes quite giggly at the thought of it.

CHAPTER TWENTY-FOUR

Lean, leggy, snake-hipped. I saw him leave the Tube and followed as he crossed the Common.

A pretty young man with soft brown hair curling down to above his shoulders. So young. Can't be more than twenty-one at the most. He was clearly stoned. Didn't know he was about to take a trip of a different kind.

He was carrying a guitar case. A potential problem. But once he was off the green and onto the street, I suggested he put it down while he studied the map.

He smelt strongly of marijuana and booze and didn't seem to notice how close we were. I could have kissed his soft young lips and I'm not sure he'd even have noticed, but that's not what I wanted at all, far from it.

He was something special, this one and I was on fire. My heart raced. Then he bent down and I performed the perfect swoop. Mamma would have been so proud of me.

I got him in an instant. It was a given. He was so stoned and tired that he lost consciousness almost immediately.

His body went limp and it was all over in a jiffy.

I loosened those tight jeans and rolled down the Y-fronts to reveal pale almost hairless thighs and such an innocent little parcel. I sliced away and in no time they were off and in the bag.

The street was so quiet. There was just enough moonlight to see and plenty of time for me to carve a little kiss in the form of an x and a P just beside his missing parts. I couldn't resist.

When I left, I removed it from its case and placed his instrument across his body and posed him as though he was playing. Better off as he is, he can now play to his heart's content. Right there on a pavement, another easy find.

CHAPTER TWENTY-FIVE

DI JO POLLITT

While Dr Flynn takes tapings from exposed body surfaces, uppermost surfaces of clothing and areas he suspects contact may have taken place, outside the tent I take account of the surroundings. At least it is late enough and at this time of year easy to see at 6.20am. The weather is kind, the sun is up and the temperature warm enough.

A completely residential street, anyone could have caught him at it, but it is a cul-de-sac, so not many would have been around. Still, it's a reckless murder that's for certain.

I stand on a pavement on the corner of Dulner Road, a short street lined with cherry trees in bloom and other trees fronting rows of bow-fronted red-brick Victorian two-storey houses with neat front gardens and low walls.

Courtney Street crosses the end of the road where I am standing with more similar houses, old tiled paths leading to their covered porches that frame solid, partially-glazed, painted front doors. I feel racked with tiredness as I hang about waiting for Edward to finish his examination of the body. I have been there since the call came in around 5.45am.

A milkman doing his rounds found the body. Yet another

young man murdered in the same manner as the others, except that this time a guitar, removed from a case that was lying nearby, has been laid across the body, the boy's arms moved to look as though he was playing it.

Another new thing, the top half of his clothing has been torn open and a tiny inch-high x along with the initial P have been carefully carved into the top of his left thigh just to the left of where his genitals are missing. This is spooky, to say the least. It does not escape me that my surname begins with P, but I dismiss that as unlikely since I know psychopaths, such as this clearly is, are vain and that the P is almost certain to be their own signature. Can't be sure though.

I make sure no one is watching when I drop some calming remedy on my tongue.

Flynn takes combings of the boy's head, scrapings from underneath the fingernails of both hands and from his teeth as well as swabs from his mouth. In the deathly quiet of the morning, where the forensic officers silently work the scene, a shriek rings down the otherwise almost silent little street.

A dishevelled, distraught middle-aged woman in a pale-blue dressing gown comes running down it towards the crime scene that is surrounded by red-and-white tape behind which a tent covers part of the road and all of the pavement around the body.

Two police officers close in to prevent her coming further. When it is clear she is not going away quietly I approach her. 'May I help you, madam?'

She is white-faced and her hands are shaking. 'Oh my God! Is it Rob? Oh my God! What's happened? My son's not at home. Is it him? Oh my God, oh my God! I don't know where he is. What's happened here? Tell me! Is it Rob?'

'I'm afraid we cannot let you go any further, madam. This is a crime scene and the public are not allowed beyond the taped-off area.'

'My son was supposed to come home last night. He'd been out playing with his band but he hasn't slept in his bed. I'm worried sick.'

'Is it possible he stayed overnight with a friend and thought to let you know this morning?'

'Well, it's possible, I suppose, but he's always promised to let me know, however late, if he ever stays out and he always has. I bought him a, a mobile phone recently for that very purpose because he knows how worried I get.'

'How old is your son, Mrs er...?'

She is stammering. 'He's nineteen. His name is Leatham, Robin Leatham. He played at a place called The Minstrel last night in Earl's Court. They're called Pilot, the band, that is. He said he was coming home. I knew he'd be very late but when he says he's coming home he always does and he definitely would have called if he decided to stay at a friend's house.'

'Might you be able to contact his band-mates to find out where he went when the band finished playing? And er, does he play an instrument and if so, what does he play?'

I already know the answer. I take her arm, lead her away from the taped-off area and walk her gently down the street. I know it is her son. The dead boy looks about nineteen.

I ask where she lives and she points to a house near its end. I walk slowly to her door where I suggest she wakens her other son who is almost eighteen. I see the distressed woman into her house, make her a cup of tea and try to calm her. Then I tell her I'll be back shortly.

Dr Flynn is packing up his bag. I touch his arm. 'Hello Edward, how's it going? Sorry to ask at such an early stage but if you could give me the nearest possible approximate time of death? We might have a chance of finding a witness who was on the Common. There should have been a number about late at night. Also, was the boy carrying a mobile phone?'

'Hello Jo. I'd say death was roughly between 3.30am and 4.30am. And yes, we were surprised to find a mobile phone and a wallet. I mean only surprised that one so young would have one on account of the expense of such items. It's already been bagged up. You want to see it? You look exhausted. You okay?'

In spite of his close association through his work with criminals and murderers, Edward Flynn is not what I would call street-wise which I find quite endearing about him. He just doesn't have the time to concern himself with such matters. I suppose if he was more street-wise, he might not be such a dedicated and passionate forensic scientist.

He wouldn't know that nowadays quite a number of young men of Robin's age carry mobile phones, usually paid for by their middle-class parents, and judging from the house, the Leatham family are reasonably well-off. He won't have had his own car yet, I'm sure, but will probably have passed his test and occasionally be allowed to borrow his mother's.

'I'm fine. Bad night. Little sleep.'

I take the phone and leaf through the contents of the small brown wallet. His name is on a driver's licence: Robin Leatham.

I contact the office to send an FLO down as fast as possible. The news has to be broken. I dread it. Suddenly Mum flashes into my head. She is crying. That is when I have to turn away from the others and walk off a distance. I must push her image away. I have to prevent myself from cracking. I have a job to do. I need to hold it together.

I light a Camel and take some deep, long drags as I sit on the edge of a low wall bordering a front garden. I imagine myself soothing Mum until she smiles and feels better and until I feel able to carry on.

I have to face poor Robin's mother and hold it together while I do so. The crime-scene manager organises a couple of officers to put Robin in a body bag, lift him onto a gurney, wheel him into a waiting ambulance and accompany his body to St George's Hospital, Tooting where he is taken to the mortuary. His guitar and its case have been wrapped in plastic and goes with him. He remains there undisturbed in the bag for the parents to identify before Dr Flynn sees him.

The FLO arrives and we go together to break the news to the mother and brother. It is terrible. I want the ground to swallow me up. Their grief is overpowering. They both collapse – their legs literally giving out on them – and they both seem half the size they were before being told. The mother suddenly looks as frail as a sparrow.

The liaison woman is great and supports both of them as well as she can and even offers them a tot of brandy, not usually done in these circumstances, but these two really need some medicinal help. I sit with them for a while and feel racked with pity, sadness and inner rage that this could have happened.

I wonder if it will be a child next time. This is the youngest victim yet. God, we need to catch this effing madman. If we don't I think he may as well kill me. This case is doing it anyway. It's the worst I've ever worked on.

I've dealt with much worse violence than this, much worse crooks. But this is different. It is so utterly pointless. This has no cause. The usual murders are committed for greed, revenge, sexual purpose, jealousy, love, rage, some motive that has some reason, twisted maybe, but something one can just about comprehend. This killer appears to have no motive that we can understand. He doesn't even have sex with his victims. The deaths make no sense, at least not to anyone who is sane.

Later, I take Tony to be present at the identification. Rob's divorced mother and father insist on coming independently.

This seems extraordinarily sad. At such a time, cannot the parents overcome their own quarrels to come together and support one another? Instead, each one stands at separate times beside the body, privately weeping and grieving alone. I can only think there must have been another woman or man in one of their lives.

In my experience there is nothing like bitter jealousy to bring about such an inability to forgive.

CHAPTER TWENTY-SIX

DR EDWARD FLYNN, FORENSIC PATHOLOGIST

E dward and Phoebe met at medical school undergraduate
training.

They both felt they could not give children a good enough
life and with some mutual relief years back they had agreed to
forego including them in their lives in favour of their
commitment to their jobs.

There is so much to learn about bodies that it has taken
Edward sixteen years to become a fully-fledged forensic
pathologist while Phoebe, who specialises in dermatology, has
finally become a senior consultant, expert in psoriasis. She has a
well-paid job at St Thomas' Hospital in Westminster Bridge
Road in London. When she first worked as a junior skin
consultant and was on a decent salary and Edward was earning
enough as a histopathologist, they bought a fine Victorian four-
bedroom semi-detached villa in Battersea.

Edward's job as a Home Office registered forensic
pathologist working in the London Inner South Coroner's
Court area covers the boroughs of Southwark, Lambeth,
Greenham and Greenwich.

Sometimes he will be called out for court appearances

where he is expected to show up at 9am. So to avoid driving in the rush hour for ages in the morning he travels the night before to a B&B or a hotel where he will stay overnight near the court, ready for the morning appearance. Bromley, for instance, is a forty-seven-minute drive in ordinary traffic conditions. He will stay nowadays overnight in some bed and breakfast in Bromley on account of a court appearance he has to make at nine the following morning.

Some days in court, others in a hospital mortuary, sometimes in his car driving to a crime scene, Dr Flynn has a wide, densely populated area to cover in which a large number of murders take place. He is a very busy man whose endless energy serves him well.

His weeks consist of such varying events where one day might be a death from uncomplicated heart disease and a couple of cases of 'the old lady's friend' (pneumonia) killing off the aged. The next day he'll be in court half the day giving evidence and then perform three autopsies in the afternoon.

Sometimes, he'll be at crime scenes; more often in mortuaries or morgues. He might be talking to lawyers about an upcoming trial or he might be up to his elbows in intestines.

He works mostly on his own but with the support of police, procurators fiscal and coroners' officers, and mortuary staff. He's in touch with other pathologists, as well as the police, barristers and lawyers.

Now that he has the extra concern of the multiple killings playing on his mind, Dr Flynn is like a machine that never stops.

Back in St George's Hospital mortuary in Tooting, the doctor has never been so careful before when examining a corpse. This is the fourth murder and as he says to Jo, he really wants to find something to help the police. To help him concentrate, he has brought his cassette player, which is perched on a shelf. Judy Garland warbles in the background.

Using a magnifying glass, he peruses every inch of Robin's young body. He harbours the thought that he should test that these carved letters have not been a conduit for some sort of poison to enter the bloodstream. He particularly wants to examine the lungs, the stomach contents and the liver.

Having finished his exam of the outside of the corpse, Flynn now indicates he needs help to roll the body over onto its back again. His assistant obliges.

With a large, intensely sharp knife, he slowly cuts a Y-shape from shoulder-to-shoulder meeting at the breastbone and then splits open the trunk of the body, the upper part cutting carefully right down the centre to the groin, peeling back the flesh as he goes, placing the top part of the flesh over the face, the rest to the sides where he then forces open the ribcage, before cutting out the sternum with two sides of ribs still attached to it. He puts the whole thing to one side.

The lungs, heart and trachea are visible. Thick, sticky blood had pooled either side in the chest cavities. Edward lowers a large ladle to scoop the glutinous liquid into a plastic jug that he tips down a drain in the basin at the end of the metal autopsy table. Having disposed of two jugs-full, he removes the high internal organs. He places them gently on a table to one side.

Now, taking a smaller knife, he slices open and examines the trachea, then the lungs, then the heart. He doesn't feel it necessary to touch the head. He can see no reason to. He examines the stomach contents. Rob ate a steak, chips and salad plus chocolate tart and vanilla ice cream for his supper.

The doctor smiles to himself, happy that the lad had an enjoyable last meal. He would like to tell Rob's parents, but they might not appreciate it.

CHAPTER TWENTY-SEVEN

DI JO POLLITT

E ating sandwiches and drinking coffee out of proper cups
(a welcome change from the canteen plastic) in the
super's office, Delaney, Green and I have a lunchtime meeting.

Before putting out the press statement, we talk about how
the killer has gone further. In a macabre new development, the
guitar had been placed in the dead boy's arms to look as though
he was playing, like some awful grotesque.

Then the killer carved an x that Delaney is certain is
supposed to represent a kiss. The entire murder is a tease, a
tantaliser that said, 'Look, I have time to arrange my victim as I
like and even to carve this little message for you.'

That being the case, we all agree, I shall send one back to
the murderer. Together we chose certain words designed to get
under the skin.

'What I suggest we need to do,' Delaney declares in his
characteristically unrestrained manner, 'is to rankle the bastard
into making a mistake. I believe it's our best hope of catching
him or her. Agreed?'

When Delaney mentions 'her' as a possibility, Maurie goes
quite red in the face and I wonder for a horrible moment

whether he might be going to have a stroke. Damage limitation is called for. Before the Irishman can say any more, I throw Maurie a knowing look that I hope he will interpret to mean not to take the man too seriously. 'Mr Delaney thinks there is a very slim chance that the killer could be a woman, but on balance, is fairly sure he's male.'

This contains Maurie from exploding with rage at the very absurdity of such an idea. He seems to have got my meaningful expression and to my relief says nothing. At this juncture, Maurie decides he's heard enough and takes the reins. 'Okay. Let's wrap this up. We're agreed we'll put out a press statement right away that contains the wording we have decided on. I shall arrange it immediately. Thank you, Detective Pollitt, Mr Delaney.'

The headlines of the late editions of the London evening newspaper read:

THE KEEPER KILLS AGAIN!

Young male garrotted and mutilated near Clapham Common

A nineteen-year-old male, Robin Leatham, was found murdered near his home on a London street near Clapham Common in the early hours of Saturday morning. His strangled and mutilated half-naked body was discovered by a milkman just before 5.30am on Saturday.

Metropolitan Police detectives investigating the murder are appealing to the public for information on the attack, which took place in the early hours of Saturday morning.

A murder investigation has been launched and no arrests have been made so far. A post-mortem examination is being carried out at St George's Hospital, Tooting.

Leading the investigation, Detective Inspector Jo Pollitt said: 'This is yet another savage murder that has heartlessly ended a young man's life. The person committing these killings is clearly suffering from a mental illness that must be hard for them to bear. They should hand themselves in to the authorities where they will be offered psychiatric help, treatment and understanding. If they can do this, it will be taken into consideration.

'Meanwhile, if there are any witnesses who may have seen Robin leaving Clapham South Tube station and crossing Clapham Common between the hours of 3am and 5am on Saturday morning or who saw anyone suspicious in the area at that time, please would they come forward as soon as possible.

'And if you think you may know who could be responsible for this latest or any of the previous murders but are afraid to come forward, we can assure you your call will be treated in the strictest confidence. These terrible murders must be stopped. Please do call.'

The telephone number is printed below the piece.

This evening at about 2213, Tony drives us to an address in South Kensington. We park nearby and walk up some steps to a grand porch where I lift a heavy, gleaming, brass lion's head knocker to let it fall on a large, thick, glossy, black front door.

After a while, the door slowly opens a few inches and the smartly coiffured auburn head of a woman peers through the gap above a thick brass chain between the door and its frame.

'You are?'

'Good evening, madam. It's the South London Metropolitan Police here. Does Miss Alexandra Wilmot-Farquhar live here, please? We spoke earlier regarding an interview with her.'

'You don't look like police. How do I know you are?' Her voice makes every word she says sound as though she is not only certain of her superiority but is also totally disapproving of just about everything at the same time.

My hackles are standing bolt upright. Police badge already in my hand I bring it close to the chain. The woman peers at it for some time.

'So is Alexandra there, please?' I am becoming impatient.

'Just a moment, I'll tell her you're he-ah.' She pauses and stares at us rudely. 'You're very late. Wait thah.'

She shuts the door again. We are left standing outside a five-bedroom house on a street in an exclusive area called the Little Boltons where houses sell for between one and two million pounds. We look at one another and I whisper, 'And they called us at twenty past nine! Obviously not a police-loving family then. And who would have thought? Think you'll be the first ever black person inside this house?'

'Apart from slaves. In this century I reckon I will, ma'am.' He does his squeaky giggle.

The woman returns to the door, unlatches the chain, opens the door and allows rather than invites us in. 'I am Lady Wilmot-Farquhar. Yar names? Why are you not in uniform?'

If this rude, stiff, po-faced woman is going to be like that with us, I shall show her what rude, stiff and po-faced really is. I stand tall and look down my nose at the small woman who is forced to bend her head back to look up at me.

Sarcasm edges my words. 'I am Detective Inspector Pollitt of the Metropolitan Police,' I gesture at Tony, 'and this is Detective Sergeant Smith. We are plain-clothes detectives who work in the criminal investigation department, commonly known as the CID. Perhaps you may have heard of it? We are conducting an urgent inquiry into a homicide and unfortunately do not have time to waste.'

I deliberately pause, fix the woman in the eye and add slowly as though it's an afterthought, 'Madam.' I pause again. 'You called us earlier this evening with regard to some information relating to the murder of one Robin Leatham that Miss...' I glance at my notes – not an easy name but what would you expect around here – 'Alexandra Wilmot-Farquhar has offered to divulge to us. We are here to see Alexandra. Where is she please?'

'She's this way. Follow me. She is my daughter. But I need you to understand that the poor darling has been extremely upset by this terrible news.'

'I have no doubt she will have been. But I am a very experienced officer and can assure you I will take the very greatest care with my words.'

This awful woman, who wears a camel-coloured cardigan over a cream silk blouse, pearls at her neck, the blouse tucked into a fitted, straight, brown dog-tooth skirt and brown court shoes, leads the way. When we reach a closed door, she slips off her shoes and asks us to remove ours with no explanation. Tony and I baulk with surprise but we do as she says with no questions asked. I have no time for confrontation with this awkward bitch. We've enough on our plates.

She opens the door to an unexpectedly large sitting room with a thick white carpet. Three enormous white sofas with plum, purple and pink satin and silk cushions range around a large open fireplace with an ornate black marble mantlepiece. A large glass chandelier hangs in the centre while pink, purple and white swag and tail pelmets with huge long fringes hang over massive thick chintz curtains that are closed across a bay window. Ostentatious plum tasselled tie-backs hang either side of them on pale-pink walls. I have never seen such a carefully styled room that somehow manages to end up looking so second-rate. It's all about money and little about class.

A pretty, slim girl with long streaked blonde hair and large dark eyes is draped across one of the sofas. She lies in a provocative pose. Her face is tear-stained, her heavy eye make-up smudged. Although she looks the worse for wear, she has still carefully arranged herself ready for her audience. We can see straight away she likes attention.

I introduce Tony and myself and ask what she can tell us about the previous night.

Her mother sits down on an armchair next to the sofa.

'I'd prefer to talk to Alexandra on her own, if you don't mind,' I say, delaying the 'madam' again. Lady Wilmot-Farquhar frowns with annoyance but does as she is told and leaves the room, conveniently forgetting to close the door properly. I nod at Tony who walks over and quietly closes it.

Thanking the girl for calling us when she read the news about Rob's terrible murder, I encourage her to tell her story. This she manages between breathless sobs and both Tony and I reckon that although a part of her is enjoying the drama, more of her is genuinely shocked and upset. Murder is not something she is likely ever to have come across before in her privileged young life, particularly one of someone of her own age and whom she has been close to.

It is around 11pm when, grateful to leave the Wilmot-Farquhars behind us, we head home. We've learned from Alexandra that Rob Leatham had intended to catch a Tube homeward from Victoria. She has given us the phone number of the minicab company that she used to collect her from Oz's house in Chelsea. That will have to wait until the following morning.

109

When he gets to the station at 8.30am, Tony contacts the cab company Alexandra used and soon traces the taxi driver who was called to the friend's home. Shown a recent photo of Rob, he confirms that having first dropped off Alexandra in the Little Boltons, he then drove Rob to Victoria where he recalled the boy leaving the cab carrying his guitar. He saw him heading into the Tube station.

This indicates the likelihood that Rob took the Victoria line a few stops south to Stockwell where he presumably changed onto the Northern line southbound for a few more stops and then exited the nearest Tube station to his home at Clapham South. We could therefore guess a rough route the young man might have taken home across the Common, a famous place for cruising homosexuals. It is clear that both young things were mashed off their heads and Alexandra is unable to confirm the approximate time she was dropped but said she thought it had been around 3am.

The friend's father from whose house they had been hastily evacuated confirmed that he had 'invited them to leave' at about 2.30-ish.

The possibility that the murderer might either know or have some link to the victims has already been thoroughly looked into. There is such divergence in the men who were killed that it seems unlikely. But there may have been a thread and it is vital that we investigate all possibilities. I have to cover all eventualities, all may-have-beens.

After extensive interviews with the victims' families, we establish that none of the vics attended the same school, the same clubs, the same doctors, dentists, sports events. Every inch of their lives is scrutinised but no connections between any of them is found.

We are in my office. It is morning and Delaney has recently arrived.

'Well, it's looking like we have someone who loves young males.' Delaney removes his glasses, one hand with two fingers on a temple and a thumb on his cheek while the other twirls them around his fingers. 'A homosexual, I'd bet my Timberlands. The killer's getting bolder. I think the x was a kiss for you, Jo. A kind of catch me if you can.'

'You think?'

'I do. He's saying: I have the time to leave you a sign that I can do as I wish and you'll never catch me. If there's another murder, Mother Mary knows, he'll leave more carving with some other message.'

'You think it's to me, specifically? You seem so certain, Patrick.'

'It's that I feel I'm beginning to get into the psyche of this maniac. I think he's a frustrated homosexual. I haven't altogether ruled out a female yet but am leaning toward a homosexual male who cannot get the partners he wants, particularly young, virile ones. I believe he hated his father for reasons that go far back into his early childhood and I suspect that as a result he may suffer from impotence. I am also fairly certain he is not considered attractive by other men.'

I chip in, 'On the other hand, maybe he dislikes gay men. Maybe he thought his victims were gay?'

'Hmmm. Doubtful. No way would he be likely to think either Winston or Ahmad were...' He pauses. 'Well, I suppose at a pinch he might have thought Ahmad could be, but it's unlikely that he would assume Jim might be. Rob, I grant you. Pretty boy on Clapham Common late at night... but he is the only one. Listen, if he wanted to kill gay boys, he wouldn't hang out in all those different places, he'd simply go where they are.'

'Maybe the first ones were just practice. Maybe now, that he's carving kisses and growing in confidence, he is killing the ones he really wants to. The gay ones. There are just so many angles to look at this. But let's for the moment assume you're right. He only wants to kill young men and take away their crown jewels. Therefore, your theory does seem pretty likely. In fact, thinking about it, I'll check out all known homosexuals with a record of violence south of the Thames.'

'No, Jo. Just as live bodies do, dead bodies also have their own language. If there's one thing these bodies have told us is that, with the exception of the quick pain experienced when dying, they have not been hurt while alive. Remember, he doesn't like to make them suffer. We have to look at the behavioural characteristics of this killer.'

'But why doesn't he? If he resents them and is jealous of them, why don't the murders involve the usual violence and rage? Why, Patrick? Can you explain? It's what makes him so effing hard to find. If he were more aggressive, there are hundreds of possible suspects out there.'

'I wish I could explain. As you say, it's effing hard, this one, Jo. But we'll crack it.'

'Will we? I can only say I hope you're effing right, Patrick.' I only just manage a smile.

WEDNESDAY 20TH DECEMBER, 1971

CHAPTER TWENTY-EIGHT

A SCHOOLGIRL

S he was late leaving school that day as she had been helping prepare the hall for the nativity play the following day, so she caught a later bus home than usual. It was already dark and just after five o'clock by the time the number 28 came along.

The journey home, usually shared with other schoolchildren although not this time, was particularly disagreeable on account of a narrow-faced, mean-looking young man with small glittering eyes and dirty, greasy hair who sat opposite and stared at her. He kept gazing at her legs in their grey school knee socks and eyeing her face and body in a nasty kind of way and she didn't like it at all.

As the bus approached the stop where she got off, the pretty, willowy girl rapidly made her way to the rear platform where she clung to the upright bar, balancing precariously at the open end of the vehicle ready to jump off as soon as it was safe. She did this before the bus had quite stopped and half ran with it as it gradually slowed to a halt then she'd walked briskly in the direction of home leaving that horrid, seedy man far behind her. Slowing her pace as she walked, something made her glance over her shoulder and there he was. To her horror he was close behind her. She panicked and broke into a run but he caught up with her and grabbed her by an arm.

'No need to run, girl. I'm not going to harm you. I just happen to be going your way. I'll just walk along with you for a while. I mean you no harm, girl.'

He gripped her arm tightly.

'That hurts. Please let go of me. Please let go!' Becoming frantic, she looked around for someone to help but there was nobody on the street. As she opened her mouth to scream, a rough, hard-skinned hand covered her mouth and she was pulled violently along the pavement and into a nearby alleyway full of dustbins.

It was also where he took a dangerously sharp knife from his pocket, held it to her throat and whispered in her ear, 'One sound, girl, and your throat is slit from here to here.'

She felt the point of the knife skim across the skin under her chin and she felt where it nicked the skin just under the centre. This man meant what he said. It was dark here and she froze with fear, unable to do anything. Overwhelmed by terror, she was dragged further down the alley to its dead end where there was only a little ambient light from local houses but it was where he felt safe enough to cut her clothes off her young body, gag her with part of her own school shirt which he thrust painfully deep into her mouth and then rape her viciously and without mercy. When he had finished in a short time, he hit her hard in the face before he left and she was temporarily stunned. He left the child in deep shock, brutalised and bleeding.

Eventually, she came to enough to remove the shirt from her mouth and stagger to her feet. She wandered in a daze out of the alley and knocked on the nearest door where a kind woman, horrified at the state of the child on her doorstep with blood pouring down her face and torn clothing, took her in and immediately called the police.

When she told her story to a policeman, she recalled that she had actually said please when she'd asked her rapist to let go of her arm, good manners having been drummed into her as part of her upbringing. The agonising irony that she had shown such decent social behaviour toward someone who had applied the extreme opposite toward her did not strike her at the time.

All remaining childhood innocence in that fifteen-year-old virgin was savagely obliterated that day. In its place, a deep anger and condemnation took seed.

MID-JUNE TO EARLY AUGUST, 1996

CHAPTER TWENTY-NINE

DI JO POLLITT

By the middle of June, as with the previous three murders, we have found nothing to go on and no new evidence or witnesses have come forward. It is now eleven months since the first murder and the police are no nearer to finding the culprit.

The gutter press behave like rabid dogs baying at the heels of the victims' families, giving them no peace to grieve. And blame is heaped onto the Met for failing to nail the murderer.

But they leave the story alone when on 15 June the IRA bomb a street in central Manchester. They give a ninety-minute warning but the bomb squad are unable to defuse the bomb in time, and 200 members of the public are badly injured in the major blast that wrecks the street.

Delaney feels it is counter-productive to flushing out the killer, but I am desperate for help and to his disappointment the super and I contact the producers of the popular BBC TV programme *Crimewatch*. Audiences of around fourteen million watch the programme that goes out monthly and since the nation closely follows every event concerning 'The Keeper', I reason we may as well use the widest possible platform to help catch him.

The *Crimewatch* production company is only too happy to oblige, knowing their viewing figures will shoot up. They unusually decide to devote an entire edition to the subject.

While all the murder victims are named and photographs of their faces are displayed on screen, only one reconstruction is made. It is of the latest murder victim's last known movements.

With Rob's mother's help, they agree to cast a young actor as close to Rob's looks as possible. That is when his eighteen-year-old younger brother Charles, who happens to look very like him, offers to stand in as his lookalike.

Unsure about the effect this might have on the boy, the police consult a psychologist who, following a session with him, gives his opinion that it could only be beneficial in helping the bereft younger brother come to terms with his grief.

At the huge Television Centre in White City, west London, before the programme runs on Thursday 4th July, an announcement is made. 'Now follows a special edition of *Crimewatch* which is aired an hour later than usual. This programme contains scenes that some viewers may find distressing.'

A digital clock ticks over in the left corner of the screen as it always does throughout the programme, the music plays, the credits roll and *Crimewatch* is on.

In a studio full of busy people at desks, the standing male presenter speaks in solemn tones. 'Good evening. Tonight is a special edition of this programme that we have aired an hour later than usual due to the especially sensitive nature of the material and to ensure that younger viewers do not see it. This is the first time in the long-running history of *Crimewatch* that we have devoted an entire programme to the subject of one criminal. But that is because this is a criminal who must be caught. Since July last year there have been four so far unsolved murders by a serial killer on the streets of south London. I am now going to pass you over to Detective Inspector Jo Pollitt of the Metropolitan Police who is the senior investigating officer on this case.'

The presenter walks across the studio to where I am standing. My throat is dry and an image of Mum flashes into my head. She is smiling and clicking her tongue at me in her way that meant, *Don't be silly. Whatever are you worried about? You'll do fine.*

'Inspector Pollitt, would you please explain to the viewers the method behind these horrific killings and what we know so far.'

I nod and smile at the presenter. 'Certainly, thank you.' Turning to face the camera in front of me, I read from an autocue. 'As you may have read in the press or seen or heard on the newscasts over the past year, these killings have been done by someone who may be trained in or has certainly learned well the method of garrotting.

'Each victim was sprung upon from behind, we believe taken by surprise, and expertly garrotted with five-millimetre white cord that is in common use and often used as clothesline or washing line. This was knotted in the middle like this one I have here.' I hold the rope up to the camera. 'I am showing you this in the hope that it jogs someone's memory.

'If you have seen one like this and you believe it may have been used for suspicious purposes, please contact us. You can remain completely anonymous if you so wish. For now, though, please keep watching.

'The reason the cord was knotted in the middle was in order to enable the killer to crush the larynx while strangling the victim thus disabling the vocal cords. This meant the victims could not cry out.' I long for a cigarette. I haven't been allowed to smoke in the TV studio earlier while I was waiting.

I pause, an old trick of mine used often for effect. I look down at the floor in front of me. Then, head still down, I raise only my eyes to the camera. 'Once the victim was down, the murderer emasculated them.'

I wait a few seconds for those who understand the word to take it in, then for those who do not, to hear me say, 'He or she took a knife and removed the genitals.'

Again I allow silence to play opposite me. I know its effect so well. I can tell from the mesmerised look of the studio technicians and the rest of the programme makers in the studio that the appeal is working well. I continue, 'I say he or she, because we have not entirely ruled out the possibility that these killings were committed by a female. Black PVC fibres have been found at the scene of each crime and we are not yet sure where they come from. We do know that whoever committed these murders is clever. They have taken place in four different locations. Lambeth, Tooting Bec, Bermondsey and Clapham, all in south London.

'As I said, this person is clever but they are also severely mentally ill and it is essential that they are caught as soon as possible. Shortly, you will hear from the bereaved relatives of the victims and you will see a film reconstruction of the latest murder. I would ask you please to pay great attention to what you are about to see and hear and to let us know if there is anything, anything at all you think you may have witnessed or overheard.

'Maybe you saw someone, or someone you know came back late at night on one of the nights in question and seemed to be acting suspiciously? Anything that you think might be relevant to our enquiries, please contact the number that you can see on the screen now. You never know, it could lead to an arrest.'

The camera pans back to the presenter who thanks me for my contribution and speaks briefly about how shocked everyone must feel having heard what I had to say.

The presenter then says, 'Well, if you do know anything that you think can help, just make that free call to the number on the screen.'

The presenter repeats the number and also gives the number of the Southwark Police Branch.

Interviews are then shown with relatives of the victims that are intercut with photos of the victims smiling in happy times. This makes the programme all the more compulsive and heart-rending. It starts with Sandrene talking about the tragedy of the loss of her beloved husband and how hard life has become for her and her young children. Then one of Ahmad's brothers takes the place of his heartbroken parents to talk about the death of his sibling.

The reality of how wide the killer spreads his net from Lambeth to Tooting is emphasised. A real old East Ender, Jim Hayden's father is perhaps the most moving as he talks about the hopes he'd had for his young boy. His struggle and failure not to weep in front of the cameras is hard to watch.

Lastly, Rob's mother addresses the camera with teary eyes about how he played guitar since he had begged to be given one aged eleven and how good he had become at it and how dedicated he was to both writing songs and singing. She speaks about the high ambitions he had for his band and how hard they had rehearsed and the gigs they had played in London and the following they were gaining.

The film then cuts to a staged reconstruction of Rob's band leaving the gig at the Minstrel in Earl's Court. The drama includes imagined dialogue with actors as the cameras follow 'Rob' and a few friends to where they went to their friend's house in Chelsea and then later of how 'Rob' and 'Alexandra' took a taxi to her home in the Little Boltons where she had been dropped off and where Rob had continued in the cab to Victoria Underground Station to catch the Tube home.

Charles Leatham is now followed by the cameras dressed as his brother carrying a guitar case in his right hand as his brother always did. He walks to the ticket office at Victoria Underground Station where he buys a ticket. The cameras track him as he takes a Tube southbound on the Victoria line to Stockwell where he then changes onto the Northern line southbound and waits for a train. He rides four stops to Clapham South. There he is seen leaving the Tube station and crossing Clapham Common. The film is intercut with photographs of Rob's face while the commentary asks if anyone remembers seeing him on the Tube, leaving it or crossing the Common on his last journey. He particularly stood out, the commentator reminds them, because he carried his guitar case.

The murder is described as savage and the killer as psychotic – the same description the police had used before in an attempt to goad the killer into turning himself in. The commentary asks people if they knew anyone who they believe is mentally unwell and who has been behaving suspiciously in the past year or who they know was out very late that night.

At the end of the programme the presenter once more emphasises how vital it is that the murderer is caught before 'this out-of-control person' kills again.

The presenter signs off by saying, 'The police are advising people in south London not to leave their homes between midnight and daylight until this maniac is caught. Please do listen to the police advice, and thank you for watching. Don't have nightmares, do sleep well.'

I leave the studio as soon as I am able and drive home where the first thing I do is to pour myself a large gin and tonic – no time to make a cocktail tonight, it's too late and I'm exhausted.

My mobile rings. It is the super, who has, of course, made sure to watch the programme.

'Well done, Jo. You spoke very well indeed. I think we'll get a lot of interest and info from viewers. This could give us the breakthrough we've been hoping for. Good job, girl. Proud of you. Now we can sit back and wait for the calls to come pouring in.'

Maurie congratulating me? Jo? Am I hearing things? Is he drunk? I can hardly believe it. He must have gone soft in the head.

The following morning Edward Flynn calls.

'Very well done, Jo. You really sold it to the public last night. Congratulations. I think you'll get somewhere with people calling in. I was pleased you mentioned the possibility of the suspect being female. I have wondered about this for some time, with an increasing feeling that this is a possibility. The black PVC has puzzled me, as no doubt it has you, for some time. I wondered whether the fibres might be from one of those PVC raincoats that my wife says she has seen girls wearing. Phoebe believes they are fashion items. Heaven forbid they're anything else. Anyway, that little carved x almost confirmed what I was wondering before. I think that is a feminine thing to do. Agree?'

'I suppose now you mention it, perhaps it is. I mean, I can't say that for certain but I see what you're saying, Edward.'

'I've wondered whether it might be a woman none too attractive to men, perhaps unable to find a boyfriend. Maybe as a result, men have become the objects of her anger.'

'Hmm. Possibly. I'll think about it. Thanks for the call, Edward. You're always so encouraging and full of good ideas. I'll talk it through with Delaney who has said all along he thinks it could be a female.'

'He's a good profiler, Jo. Been right on a lot of cases.'

'He is and he has.'

'Well, work calls as always. Must get on. Good to chat and well done again. You did a sterling job on the TV.'

On Friday evening, Cilla and I sit cuddled up on the sofa to watch *Crimewatch* together on my video recorder. She watches in horror when she realises the reality of what her friend, who plays these things down to her, faces on a daily basis.

While we watch, she takes my hand in hers and puts her head on my shoulder. She wants me to know I have someone who cares about how I must feel having to deal with the macabre horror this killer is inflicting not only on his victims but on so many others as well.

She is evidently shocked when Jim Hayden's father talks about his loss and when she hears how young the latest victim was. But when the programme ends, she gives me some strongly positive feedback and tells me how incredibly well I am doing and what a great idea it was to turn to *Crimewatch* and how she's certain the programme will help us catch the monster. Her input is more needed by me than even she realises.

CHAPTER THIRTY

DI JO POLLITT

The information centre is set up at Scotland Yard purely to deal with calls relating to this case and the police had no idea how inundated it would become. The large number of officers working on the calls have sifted through the least likely to the most promising. Although a large number lead us up the expected blind alleys, some who claim to have seen Rob are followed up and prove correct. They are all recorded. A few more from people who may have seen the killer look promising.

When three calls come in from unrelated sources naming the same man, we prick up our ears. On the Friday after the broadcast, a call came in.

'Hallo? Is that the Metropolitan Police? And am I speaking to the information centre regarding the *Crimewatch* programme on Thursday night this week?'

The young police officer answers carefully, 'Yes, it is. PC John Adamson here. Do you have any information to share with us?'

'We-ll now,' an exaggerated drawl replies, 'I do indee-ed.'

'May I have your name please, sir?' asks the constable.

'Oh, I'd really rather not, if you don't mind, but I can

promise you that what I'm about to tell you is God's truth and you boys should *definitely* follow up on it.'

'Right, what do you have to tell me, sir?'

'We-ll, there's this foreign man known as Marco who "likes the boys" and is quite often seen "cruising" on Clapham Common. And I just happened to be walking home myself the night of that horrendous murder of that poor darling young boy and I spotted this Marco carrying a shopping bag. Well now, I *have* to say, I *do* feel he was acting suspiciously. He kept looking left and right and over his shoulder, you know, as though he didn't want anyone to see him, if you know what I mean.'

The second call is also from a gay man who is prepared to give his name and says he was 'crossing' the Common late that night at about half past three in the morning and spotted a weird character he knows as Marco who is sometimes seen around there. Apparently, he was carrying a bag and acting strangely.

A third positive call comes from a Mrs Ruby Allan who resides on the ground floor of a private block of flats on the borders of Vauxhall and the Oval.

'He lives in the flat next door, a Spanish or Italian chap, I'm not sure but he's one of those what I call queer ones, you know. I know him slightly to say hello to. He's what I'd call a loner who never has no one round but I knows he was out late that night as I was awake worrying about my pussycat who hadn't come in that evening, so I'd only slept light and when I'd heard the front door go at about 3.45, I knew it was that time because I'd looked at my watch. I'd slipped on my dressing gown and peeped out to see who it was and if anyone had by any chance let the cat in.

'But it had been that Mark chap and he'd looked ever so embarrassed to be seen you know and was acting what I'd call suspicious and carrying a shopping bag he hadn't wanted me to see and I just thought his behaviour was strange. And then when I saw the programme, well, I put two and two together and I was certain it was the same day as the murder as it was the night of my sister Ivy's birthday on May 17th and I'd been round hers and we'd got on the old Joanna and had had a good old sing-song.'

A detective has been to visit Ruby and the report has presented as one of the most likely leads going. The police have run the man's name through their records to discover that a Marco Rossi of the same address in Vauxhall has had one previous conviction for an act of gross indecency in a public toilet, for which he had been imprisoned for six months and released after four.

On a separate charge he had also been accused of molesting a fifteen-year-old boy in a train carriage but had denied it. On that occasion, according to the boy, he and the Italian had got chatting, swapped names, then Marco had started to grope his private parts.

The lad had then run out of the carriage and down the train to find the ticket collector. By the time they had returned to the carriage there had been no sign of the man. The boy had contacted police later who had visited Rossi to put the charge to him but his denial and the lack of witnesses and evidence had meant that the charge had been dropped and no further action had been taken.

On the Monday afternoon, Delaney and I visit Ruby Allan. We want to hear her story and check out the flats where Rossi lives. When we meet her, we are quite surprised at how sound and sensible she is and end up listening carefully to what she says.

'While I'm not one to tell tales on people, I can't help admitting I've always wondered about Mark, you know. I know people have a perfect right to keep themselves to themselves as he does, but he does keep such funny hours, you know and he doesn't seem to have a friend in the world and it's obvious the poor soul's what these days they call gay, you know. You can tell from how he walks and what he wears and all that, you know. He's foreign, you know. Not very good at English, either. Oh, but he's a strange one. I hear him moving about in his flat sometimes at three or four in the morning. Goodness knows what he's doing in there. He doesn't look happy, either. I don't wonder he hasn't any friends.'

'This is very helpful, Mrs Allan. We have also had a couple of other calls which we think may be regarding the same individual, only they called the man Marco. Do you think it might be the same person?'

'Well, he is foreign, that's for sure. I thought he was Mark but I really don't know. He's never corrected me when I've called him by that name.'

'Would you have any idea whether Mark or Marco has a job?'

'Well, actually I think he may do but only in the afternoons if he does. He goes out each weekday from about lunchtime and comes back about 8.30 in the evenings but I've no idea where he goes. I've tried talking to him you know. He's just not the type that wants to talk and I gave up trying some time ago. I still always say hello, mind. He says it back. Mind, I don't think he knows much of our language.'

I thank her and ask her whether she thinks Rossi might be home at present. She says she knows he isn't as she saw him leave earlier when she was checking her mailbox.

'You have given us some very interesting and helpful information and we will follow through on this. Should anything come of it, we will let you know in due course. In the meantime, we suggest you keep away from Mr Rossi and should you hear him either leave or return to the premises late at night, please stay in your own flat and call me on this number.'

I scribble down my own mobile number on her notepad and hand the torn off piece of paper to the woman. I ask her please to only call if she feels it is necessary. As we leave, we ask her to point out where Mr Rossi lives.

She shows us how close number three is to hers.

Before we leave the building, I check the mailbox for number three in the hallway. There is what appears to be a bill addressed to an M. Rossi.

Once outside, Delaney and I discuss our talk with the old lady and I tell him I am planning on bringing the man in for questioning the following morning. While Delaney is delighted and can't wait to see this character and whether he fits with his idea of the killer, I feel more circumspect. Ruby's words repeat in my mind, *'Oh, but he's a strange one.'*

We decide to search his flat while we are at it and I put in for a search warrant when I get back to Southwark while Delaney takes the underground back to Camden Town.

Once back at the station, knowing forewarned is forearmed I set a team to research as much about Rossi's background as they can possibly dig up.

I go and see Maurie to tell him we might have a lead with some Italian bloke. I can almost see his heart lifting. He stands up and nearly hugs me. I know how important this case is to him. He wants the glory of catching The Keeper before he retires.

'Yes, bring the bugger in, bring him in right away, Jo. Well done. Brilliant work.' He gives me a big smile and even winks at me before I leave the office.

This is remarkable. *Brilliant work*. Unheard of. He usually only says things like that once someone is locked up after the court case. These days he only ever calls me Jo when he is in an exceptionally good mood. It means that for now he has something to feed the press and the public who are desperate for some news.

Taking Tony, another detective sergeant called Ed Freeman and a couple of armed police constables with me, I set off the following morning, a Saturday, at 7.10am to pay Marco Rossi a surprise visit and bring him in for questioning.

We ring his doorbell four times before he opens the door.

Marco Rossi

It is warm weather and Rossi is sleeping in the buff. He doesn't have a dressing gown and he isn't used to visitors at any hour let alone as early as this. He stumbles out of bed, finds yesterday's T-shirt, grapples his way into it and without bothering with underpants, which he seldom wears anyway, he pulls on a loose pair of jeans.

Rubbing his eyes, he makes his way to the door.

Two plain-clothes men, one tall woman and two uniformed police officers crowd the hallway outside his door. The woman holds a warrant badge in his face and introduces herself and the others.

He feels instantly nervous. What are the police doing here? What do they want?

'Robin Leatham, young man, murdered near Clapham Common, early one Saturday morning in May, remember Marco?'

'I don't know, I mean... I was no there. Not at Common. Never murder nobody.'

'Of course you weren't and of course you didn't, Marco.' The woman knows his name. She dominates the door space. 'We'll just come in, if you don't mind, and you can get yourself properly dressed and we'll get on down to the station, okay?'

'And what I say I no go?'

'Then,' says the tall woman, 'we arrest you for being uncooperative with the police. Much easier just to come along now, don't you think?'

He is dumbfounded as well as nervous as hell and feels deeply uneasy. Admittedly he has been asleep so has not had a chance to make himself presentable. Granted, the nervousness will be worse on account of his rude awakening and on account of who they are.

'But I no murder nobody. I no know this man you speak about.'

'We can discuss that down at the station, can't we? In the meantime we'd like to have a look around. We do have a search warrant, okay?'

She waves the warrant in front of his face and leads him to a sofa where she sits down next to him on one side and gestures to one of the policemen to sit on the other. She then nods to the two other PCs who start a systematic search of his small, ground-floor two-bed council flat.

They search everywhere. Under the bed, they find a washing line of white cotton cord.

Then, hidden at the back of Marco's wardrobe they find a navy shopping bag containing some two-foot-six-inch-long strips of the same cord found under the bed. It also contains a Swiss Army knife, some latex gloves, a hand-held cassette recorder, some headphones and a head-torch. Freeman brings it over to the woman. When she sees it, she nods at the PC.

'Cuff him, please.'

She turns to Marco who has now been pulled to his feet and has his hands cuffed behind his back. She formally arrests him as under suspicion of murder and he starts to shake. Tears fill his eyes and fall down his face. 'I murder nobody. I never murder nobody. I never kill nobody. I tell you. I explain you.'

DI Jo Pollitt

I study the man. Wearing what is clearly a fake tan, he has

black hair and dark eyes and an over-muscled body. His thick-set, square-shaped face with its too large nose and small eyes under arched eyebrows give him a kind of supercilious air.

There is something definitely scary about him. No wonder the other gay men don't like him. He'd be considered one to avoid in their community. He looks like the kind who could enjoy hurting people. I put a signal up to my train of thought and annoyed with myself, remember about books and covers and knowing better than that.

I have never arrested a single murderer yet who has not said much the same as this man. Ignoring him, I put on some latex gloves provided by one of the constables and study the contents of the shopping bag while the constables now stand either side of Rossi.

'Bag this up please and let's get this man back to the station. Sumner, can you remain behind and seal off the flat, please. I'll send someone to collect you, okay?'

It is 8.07am. I tell Tony to go on with Freeman and the prisoner and wait in the car.

While they wait, I knock gently on the door of number two and before long, it is answered by Ruby Allan wearing her dressing gown.

I explain that we have arrested Rossi and are taking him back to the police station in Southwark. I thank her again for her help and tell her she can sleep soundly now he has gone. I tell her we'll keep in touch to let her know future developments.

When I open the car door and glance at Rossi, I am pleased to note his hands are shaking. Always better to let the prisoner sweat a bit, which is exactly what this one is doing.

As I get into the car next to Tony who is driving, I feel a sudden surge of anger. How dare this nasty piece of work go around hurting and killing others? In my head, I go over the questions I'll ask in the interview. I'll put this character through the mill. The cassette recorder? What did he use it for? I can't wait to have a listen to the tape inside it. And the head-torch? Presumably to keep his hands free for murder on a dark night.

Tony tells me later that he has been experiencing a similar feeling. He is repulsed to be at such close quarters to someone who more than likely has deliberately set out to kill four innocent people who have done nothing to him except cross his path.

CHAPTER THIRTY-ONE

DS TONY SMITH

A strong sense of justice was Tony's main reason for joining the force and he is quite often disappointed by the amount of corruption and quantity of 'bent' coppers there are that make it hard for the straight ones like himself to do their job. It is hard not to get involved with those people. Saying no to them makes you a target and there are many times he has wanted to resign and walk away.

But something makes him stay. Like his Pappa always said, he is stubborn as a mule, that boy. He doesn't want to give up all the hard work he's gone through to become a detective because of the rotten apples in the cart. There are still enough good ones struggling to do the job well, him being one of them.

For example, DI Pollitt. Now she is a woman he looks up to. She's good at her job and works her arse off to do things the right way and he is determined to help her all the way. And this one they have here in the car today, they're going to get him, for sure. As he drives into the station car park a shiver of excitement runs through him. They have caught The Keeper. They have got him with them right now and he is going to prison for the rest of his rotten life.

Marco Rossi

It is about ten past nine when Tony Smith and Ed Freeman each holding one of Rossi's arms, lead the cuffed prisoner, still trembling and head hanging, and walk him into Southwark police station where they take him to the custody reception desk. There they wait unspeaking.

The custody sergeant sighs as he looks at Marco, takes a form from a shelf, grabs a plastic bag and a ballpoint pen and without so much as glancing at the man, a definite air of boredom in his voice, takes his details.

It is only now that Marco is read his rights and told he can speak to a legal representative of his own choice or use the police duty solicitor scheme, free if he has none of his own.

Marco's body starts to shake with sobs. He wants to tell them that he usually calls his mother in Italy every Saturday. He'll have to get a solicitor who can call her and tell her he is there for some traffic misdemeanour or something. This is when he asks for a solicitor through the police. And this is when they stall calling one.

DI Jo Pollitt

Careful to wear latex gloves, in my office I check Rossi's tape is rewound to the beginning and press play. A crackling sound emerges but nothing more. This continues for twenty minutes until the tape ends. Disappointed, I turn it over and play the other side. Same again. A blank tape. I've wasted a frustrating forty minutes listening to zilch. The man must have hidden some others somewhere in his flat. Along with the trophies? They will have to pull the place apart and try to find them.

I arrange this now, while we have him in custody. Lighting up, I take a long drag. I long to discover what Rossi has recorded. The victim's last words? Because the deaths would have been relatively silent, I cannot imagine what the tapes would have been for. But no doubt he will have had some dark reason for it.

And I shall find out what it is because I am going to break this man down. I organise a team to go over to Rossi's flat and search through the place with a fine-tooth comb, if necessary, pulling down stud walls.

That done, to prevent her being frightened, I put in a call to warn old Ruby Allan that this is going to happen.

It is after 2pm that I head for Maurie's office. I knock a bright rat-a-tat.

'Come in.'

'Afternoon, sir.'

'Hello, Jo.' He leans forward in his chair, an eager look on his face. 'How did it go?'

I explain that we have arrested Rossi under suspicion and that we've found the shopping bag in his flat. Maurie looks excited and his cheeks go pink. He wants to know what we saw and what I think about the prisoner. Honestly, his face has not looked this bright for some time and is wreathed in smiles.

'Tremendous work, Jo. Just make sure you make it stick. I'll arrange a press release this afternoon. Terrific work. At last we've got something positive. But as I say, just got to make it stick.'

'I'll do my best, Maurie.' It's on occasions like this that we become equal colleagues again, he knows it and enjoys the feeling as much as I do – just like the good old days. 'Well', I say, 'better press on – must prepare for the interview.'

'Indeed. Let me know when. I'd like to be in on it.'

'Course I will. Letting him stew for a bit.'

'Tell me, Jo, do you think he's our man?'

'I think he's a strong possibility.' For a second, doubt flickers across my mind. I tell myself I must remember to include uncertainty in my thinking and am annoyed with myself for so easily forgetting. It's too easy to be sure.

We nod smiling goodbyes. I discover later on that Marco has

asked for a solicitor, which is delayed by our boys but, of course, honoured.

CHAPTER THIRTY-TWO

DI JO POLLITT

The men I've sent to Rossi's flat return with nothing. I am immediately downcast. I was so sure they'd find something. I question them rigorously. Did they cut open the mattress and pillows? Yes. Did they pull out all the kitchen appliances and check behind and under them? Yes. I sigh heavily and put my head in my hands to rack the sore old brains. He must have stored his trophies somewhere other than in his property. But where? I am determined to find out where those trophies are.

Delaney joins me.

His teasing jocularity is part of what makes Delaney charming and actually helps keep a lightness in both of us when dealing with the depths of nastiness as we are. Like many who work in dark professions, jokes between us help lift the atmosphere and I am thankful for his cheerfulness which tends to help prevent me from reacting the other way. I light a cigarette. My mother is watching me quietly. I can feel her.

'Not good for you, not good for you...' Delaney chants in a parrot voice... 'but you know that... you know that.'

'One day, I'll do something about it.' I change the subject.

We discuss what we are thinking for a time and the more we think about it, the more we both become convinced Rossi is our man. But there are still a few pressing questions. The trophies? And there are no signs of black PVC. What is the cassette recorder used for? Is there enough circumstantial or indirect evidence to get a conviction? The answer to the last question is quite clear. Without a confession, no chance.

'Come on then, Patrick. Let's get to it.'

I set the wheels in motion and Rossi and his solicitor make their way to the interview room. Delaney and I watch our man's arrival from behind the two-way mirror. He looks exhausted and frightened, like a beaten man. A police constable stands in the corner of the room.

Carrying a briefcase and knowing it makes me seem more intimidating, I hold my head high, walk tall and enter the room, Delaney is close behind me. I stride up to the table and look down on Rossi who is forced to crane his neck to look back at me.

'Hello again, Marco.'

I address the solicitor. 'Hello George, how have you been keeping? Well, I trust?' I shake hands with the man who has jumped to his feet and introduce him to Delaney. Towering over Rossi, I continue, 'I hope we've been looking after you all right? Had some lunch, Marco?'

'Yes, madam, thank you.'

'To your liking?'

'Yes, madam.'

'Good.' I gesture towards Patrick.

'This is Mr Delaney who is helping us with our investigation.' I sit down opposite Rossi and Delaney takes the chair next to mine. As I place the briefcase flat on the table to my left, I nod at DS Freeman who is standing by the cassette recorder.

'Uncuff Mr Rossi please, constable. Thank you.' The constable steps forward and does so. Rossi has been manacled for most of the day except he had them removed while he had been given some sandwiches for his lunch. No knives or forks allowed in case he tried anything. But when he's eaten, they've been re-attached. Removing them now is part of my strategy. A small part of me feels sorry for this man, but I cannot allow this to enter my thinking.

'Smoke?' I lean across the table to offer him an extended cigarette from my pack of Camels.

'*Si. Graz...* Yes, thank you, madam.' Rossi takes the cigarette in shaking fingers, puts it between his lips. I extend my hand holding my Zippo, flame flickering and the man sucks his cigarette alight, gulping the nicotine into his lungs. The constable places the ashtray between us. DS Freeman presses the record button on the tape recorder.

'The following interview is taking place at the Metropolitan Police Southwark Police Station commencing at,' he glances at a clock on the wall, '4.38pm on Saturday 13th July, 1996. Present are the prisoner, Marco Rossi of 3 Rowan Court, Vauxhall; Detective Inspector Joanna Pollitt, Metropolitan Police, Southwark Branch; Mr Patrick Delaney, offender profiler; Mr George Hardy, solicitor for the prisoner and me, DS Edward Freeman, Metropolitan Police, Southwark Branch.'

'Now then,' I begin, 'Mr Rossi, I see from your police record that you've been arrested and charged before. Is that correct?'

'Yes, madam. It is.'

'Then you will know that this interview is being recorded and that the contents of this interview can be used as evidence against you in criminal court.' I caution him and continue in a conversational tone as though it were the sort of thing I would say to my milkman in the morning. 'You know that you are here because you have been arrested on suspicion of the murder of

Robin Leatham in Dulner Road close to Clapham Common on the early hours of May 18th, 1996. We also have reason to believe you may have committed three other murders dated July 15, 1995; January 5, 1996 and March 28, 1996. What do you have to answer to these charges?'

'I no guilty. I kill nobody.'

'Right. Firstly, were you on Clapham Common on the night of May 17th and early morning hours of May 18th this year?'

'No, I was not there.'

I sigh heavily. 'Two witnesses saw you there at around the time of Mr Leatham's murder. And you were seen returning to your flat soon afterwards carrying a shopping bag and you seemed to want to avoid being seen. So I ask you again. Were you on Clapham Common that night?'

'I forget, I go for walk there that night.'

'Oh right. Glad you remembered that after all. And why would you go for a walk there, I wonder? Especially at that hour? Bit of a way from where you live, isn't it? Often go for walks on Clapham Common late at night and in the early hours, Marco?' I am trying to keep the tone light. There's no easy rule for telling a stressed-out innocent person from a criminal who is nervously trying to trick you.

I listen to suspects in the interrogation room, then go out to begin the real work. The interrogation is the icing on the cake. I never base my case solely on what any suspect says.

When facing off with a suspect, I tend to try to get them to tell, explain and describe. It's a way of encouraging someone to tell their story. Then later, get them to repeat the story to see if they get lost and confused in the details.

Rossi says nothing but looks scared. Keeping my tone light, I turn to Delaney. 'Got it with you, haven't you, Mr Delaney?'

'I do indeed.' First putting on a pair of white latex gloves, Delaney then reaches under the table and like a magician producing a rabbit from a hat with a flourish, pops the shopper found in Rossi's flat onto the table.

'Shall we look at the contents? I think Marco's solicitor would be interested in seeing this evidence.' He empties the shopping bag and carefully spreads the contents on the table.

My tone sharpens.

'Now then, Marco. We'd just like you to explain to us your purpose in keeping these various objects in a bag at the back of your wardrobe. First, the six lengths of two-foot-six-inch white cord, which for the record are an exact match for the fibres found buried in the neck of Robin Leatham's corpse. It is a readily available five-millimetre cord often used for washing lines. What are they for?'

Rossi has gone pale when he sees the contents of the bag. So has his solicitor. It's clearly the first he has heard about it. Rossi is about to speak when his solicitor nudges him and whispers in his ear. Rossi then nods and says, 'No comment.'

'I think you were about to give us an answer, Marco, and I am impelled to warn you that your defence case may be damaged if you continue to make no comment.'

I lean across the table.

Before the solicitor can say anything, Rossi is speaking again. Accessing his brain to think of an answer, his eyes blink and flicker to the right and he says, 'For tying things on my scooter.'

The solicitor exhales loudly and whispers again in his client's ear. But Rossi carries on answering the questions. My warning has scared him more than his solicitor has managed to.

'Then why was the bag at the back of your wardrobe along with a cassette recorder, headphones, a head-torch, a Swiss Army knife and some medical gloves?'

Delaney watches him like a hawk. At this question the man's nostrils flare and although I cannot see it, I can tell from the slight tremble on the right side of his body that his right foot is jiggling under the table.

'Torch if scooter break down.'

'What is the cassette recorder for?'

'For listen music.'

'So can you explain why it had a blank tape in it?'

'For record music.'

The solicitor is clearly in despair. He tries to intervene. 'Excuse me, but I really must ask my client for a word in private. Mr Rossi, please listen to what I have to say to you.'

'Why keep it in a shopping bag?' I persist.

'For play music on scooter.' Rossi is not going to listen to his solicitor. This policewoman is a nice person who seems happy with his answers

'And the Swiss Army knife?' I keep my voice sweet.

'For fix scooter if break down.'

And now for the denouement.

'The latex gloves?'

'For hands clean fix scooter.'

I look directly at Rossi. 'I put it to you that the answers you have just given me are untrue. I think, Marco, that the strips of cord were used for garrotting men. That the head-torch was used for when you had killed your victims, you then used gloves like these'– I pointed to my own and to the small packet of them on the table – 'and this blade on the Swiss Army knife...' I slowly put on a pair of white latex gloves myself then flicked a particular knife open that had been honed by someone to a particularly sharp edge and point, '... that you have clearly sharpened yourself, to slice off their genitalia which you then took away with you on leaving the scenes of the crimes.'

I notice Delaney studying the man's behaviour. Marco crosses and uncrosses his arms; he clasps and unclasps his hands, steepling them from time to time. A rapid pulse beats at the front of his neck and his breathing is fast and shallow. Delaney will be interpreting all this.

'Is no true. I kill nobody.'

'I believe you are lying, Marco. We know your family would never accept that you are gay and how difficult for you that has been. We understand what that can do to a man. We know what it has done to you.'

I am now holding the photographs I have been going to show Rossi. The man is shaking and Delaney signals me to stop. I put them away. I say, 'That's enough for today.'

Weeping, Rossi is led shuffling out of the interview room. As he goes, I manage to say sympathetically, 'See you tomorrow, Rossi. I really would advise you to think about co-operating with us, you know. It will go so much better for you if you do.'

As I stand up to leave the room, walking out beside Delaney, I can feel Mum's warmth for a few moments. It sometimes happens when the stress builds up. That I was feeling the pressure of the situation plus the lack of sleep, the anxiety it has brought with it is not in doubt and the sense that my mum is somehow with me works as a soothing mechanism.

Deep down, I know very well that my brain is compensating on my own behalf and am grateful to it, but for now I am happy to swim in its shallower waters when these events occur. Delaney senses my anxiety and puts a comforting arm around me as we walk back to my office to go through what we've learnt from the interview.

CHAPTER THIRTY-THREE

DI JO POLLITT

They shout, they yell, they scream questions at me: 'What's his name?' 'Have you caught The Keeper?' 'Has he confessed?' Their words launch into the air like rockets and rebound on the pavement with dull thuds when they hit my 'no comment' responses. As I have experienced often enough and painfully so today, that irritating little two-word phrase can be the worst enemy of the questioner and closest ally of the questioned.

It's 8.07am on Sunday when I finally manage to force my way through the crowd of journalists, photographers, TV presenters and TV cameras and squeeze through the door into the station.

The cat is well and truly out of the bag now. Like starving animals they will stay there until they've got something to tell the public.

On the superintendent's say-so we're allowed to hold Rossi a further twelve hours. Day two goes as badly as the first and again we get nowhere.

On Monday morning the case is taken to the magistrates' court where we apply for and are granted a further extension of twenty-four hours which will give us sixty hours altogether, making it two nights and three days.

By day three, we have given up trying to implicate Rossi in the first three murders and are concentrating solely on the Rob Leatham killing. Again, by lunchtime when we are getting nowhere, I have had enough.

We break for lunch and in the afternoon, I change into top gear. It's my only hope as time is running out. We can interview the guy until 8pm when we will have to let him go.

'We've got all the evidence we need, Rossi. You're the murderer; we have no doubt about that at all. You're going down for it, you know. If you admit what you did and tell us why you did it, as I've already explained a great many times,' I sigh with frustration, 'it will go a lot easier for you. Just tell us what you did with Rob's male parts.'

He looks at the solicitor who nods. 'I never kill nobody. I no know this man. I no do nothing to him.'

Now I produce the photographs of Rob's mutilated body with the carved letter P and the x in front of him. Rossi looks sick and turns his head away.

I have built up a head of steam. 'Look at it, man! Look at what you did!' I shout at the quivering man.

Still Marco refuses to look. I am close to losing it. Leaning across the table I stare into Rossi's face. I stab the photos with a furious finger. I can sense that Delaney next to me is alarmed.

Freeman speaks quietly into the recorder. 'Suspending the interview at 2.19pm.'

'Look at the effing pictures, you bastard. See how you ended that poor young man's life! And what you did to his body? His private parts. The bits he would most have cared about. You took them away from him. For what? Why? Because you felt like it? You didn't even have sex with–'

Rossi's solicitor who up to this point has remained relatively silent stands up, a hand making a stop sign in the air as a traffic cop might do.

'This is outrageous, DI Pollitt. You are bullying my client with undue cause. You have no real evidence of Mr Rossi's involvement in this case and I demand that you desist from questioning him forthwith. You have had him in here for three days to put up with your unsubstantiated accusations. You have nothing to hold him for. He has admitted to being on Clapham Common on the night of the murder of Robin Leatham, but that is all. So were many, many other people. You have no evidential proof. You are clutching at straws and you need to let this poor, nervous man go free.'

The room is quiet. I shrug and look at Delaney. He shrugs back. We are beaten and we know it. I sit down, look at the prisoner and say quietly, 'Mr Rossi, you are free to go. Detective Freeman will take you through to collect your things and will arrange transport to take you back to your home. I apologise for any inconvenience we have caused you.'

I feel myself go red with embarrassment. 'Bullying', 'unsubstantiated accusations', 'no real evidence'. My harsh words reverberate and I am shocked at myself. Has the urge to catch a killer taken me over and allowed my common decency to vanish? I am going to have to check myself daily from now on. Above everything else, I must be true to myself, or what is the point of all this?

And what if Rossi actually *is* innocent? My compulsion to make the charge stick has made me forget the possibility. I feel ashamed and small.

CHAPTER THIRTY-FOUR

DI JO POLLITT

Despondency has taken over at Southwark Police Station. On reflection, I still think it is Rossi; Patrick Delaney is sure it is Rossi; Tony Smith thinks it is Rossi; Maurice Green thinks it is Rossi; Edward Flynn thinks it is and so do all the detectives on the force. We just have to find those trophies that Delaney is certain the man keeps somewhere... but where?

I call a team meeting that includes Delaney. This afternoon we sit around brain-boxing with little progress until Tony says, 'How about a safety deposit box?'

'That's a thought... but how would he keep the genitals from decomposing?'

'Formaldehyde,' says Delaney, who comes out of his slump.

'But where would he get it from?' Tony asks.

Delaney says the chemical is used in all sorts of things including make-up. 'Where does he work, Jo?'

'At a glass-making factory. Would they be likely to use formaldehyde there?'

A quick call to Rossi's place of work tells us formaldehyde is not a chemical they use in any of their processes. Delaney says,

'We're going to have to admit defeat on this one for now. If he kills again, we'll nail him.'

The captain of the team feels the boat she has been steering has lost its rudder.

CHAPTER THIRTY-FIVE

DI JO POLLITT

In the first few days of August Patrick Delaney is thanked for his help, paid and let go. I have enjoyed and benefited from working alongside him. He has felt like an extra strength beside me and I shall miss his friendly cheek, his laughter, his positive attitude and his intelligent way of getting to the core of problems. But he has to go, of course.

As August continues, I am almost able to relax a bit. Crime is always down at this time of year and it seems we may have got the right man. But our inability to imprison Rossi means that he has literally got away with four murders. We are, of course, watching the man and whatever happens, it is unlikely he will dare to kill again, not on our patch anyway.

I console myself that if Rossi turns out not to be the killer, we would have had another by now. The previous murders had grown increasingly close together, happening less than two months apart. The killer has become increasingly impatient; the last murder was on May 18th.

Although the case is still officially open, and Maurie, furious though he is that we were unable to get Rossi to trial – so certain was he the killer had been found – is pleased with me. I am overdue a week off so plan to take it during the last week of August.

Cilla and I decide on a week in Cornwall in a good hotel close to the north coastal path. Away from the beaches and the hordes but near peace, tranquillity and beauty. Just what the doctor hadn't ordered, but what we prescribe ourselves.

Life is my work, my home, my beloved cats and Cilla, my beautiful friend who I really love.

We used to keep up a limp pretence that we were both keeping an eye out for 'Mr Right', but as time has gone by references to that idea became fewer until they have finally petered out altogether and I think both of us were silently relieved that they have.

I have no clue how Cilla might feel about Sapphic love and whether the bond we have even tends toward a physical manifestation. Perhaps it is best left as it is.

I know I have no strong lesbian tendencies toward other women and never have had. It has only ever been Cilla for me. Sexual involvement might complicate and even mess up our relationship which currently works so well and is so easy.

In truth, I myself am unsure about how I would feel about taking the plunge into such a thing. It makes me nervous to contemplate and is easier to put it off. Anyway, entrusting my gut not only when it comes to detective work but with most things, I have the impression that without yet knowing, Cilla feels the same way for me.

In the past year, we have taken to spending weekends together and Cilla usually stays with me at my house. Until now, we have not shared a bed, though we have fallen asleep on the sofa together a few late evenings after a few too many cocktails.

I've woken up in the middle of one night to realise Cilla's head is on my lap, her glasses askew on her face. Savouring this physical nearness, I've gone back to sleep, one arm resting on her shoulders.

SATURDAY AUGUST 24TH TO
THURSDAY AUGUST 29TH, 1996

CHAPTER THIRTY-SIX

JACK WILSON

It's exciting. A week before the opening, now. They say this is going to be one of the top restaurants in London. With fabulous views overlooking the river, St Paul's Cathedral and the city, the old Oxo Tower on the south bank of the Thames has undergone a complete refurbishment and on the eighth floor, the restaurant will serve the best cuisine. Alongside its set menus and the á la carte, it will feature a menu of seven courses, each with its own special wine.

On one side of it, there is an amazing outdoor terrace for people to sit and sip delicious cocktails while they watch the brilliant view across the South Bank of London while the sun sets over the capital. And this is just the weather for it. If only they were open now. But it will be soon and hopefully the weather will still be warm enough in a week's time.

Jack Wilson, Assistant Sommelier. What a title. He has been given a badge. His parents are so proud of their boy for making his way in a world that requires much learning, as well as good manners and a way with people. Wait till they see him in the outfit he's wearing for the job. Distinguished, smart. White tails, white tie and black trousers, the real McCoy.

Wine really interests Jack. He is learning on the job and at the moment they are sorting out the bottles ready for the opening. It's fascinating how much he has already gleaned. He has taken a number of courses and dreams of becoming a fully-fledged top sommelier, employed by only the best restaurants in town.

Then one day when he is older and has made a few quid he will open his own very special wine bar in the heart of Mayfair or somewhere equally posh, Chelsea perhaps, where he will only serve proper, decent wine to people who appreciate it.

There are still a number of finishing touches to be done here. The tables and chairs have not yet arrived and the cutlery is on the way. The chef is here practising dishes and sorting out his kitchen staff.

They are working shorter hours than they will be after opening and having started at eight o'clock, are allowed off at 11pm. But tonight they decide to work later so there will be less to do the next night and they will be able to get home nice and early on Saturday evening.

They carry on finishing filling the shelves with crates of various rosés, whites and Champagnes and then labelling each shelf carefully with the names and years. This takes them quite a time and they only call a halt when it's all done. And when they do finish, neither feels like going home yet. Instead, his French boss suggests they find a couple of chairs to take out onto the empty terrace.

The sommelier cracks open a bottle of one of the best of the rosé wines they have been handling today – so cheap at the price they paid but so expensive for the customers. The warm air suits it and they savour it as they gaze across London, the floodlit dome of St Paul's Cathedral dominating the view.

Nearly all the houselights are off now as it is after 3am. Stars take their place and shimmer theatrically against what looks like a blue-black backcloth behind the London skyline. A great many are out tonight. Jack knows a little astronomy and focuses on Jupiter which is looking particularly bright. He watches the planet for some time. Then he feels brave enough to say, 'What do you think of the name Jupiter for a wine bar, boss?' It runs off the tongue well. It has class. It makes sense, like a bright planet for wine-lovers to go.

'Jupiter. Hmm. For a wine bar? It's okay but I personally would prefer the name of a wine. French, of course.' He smiled. 'Why not call it,' he gestured at the bottle, 'The Whispering Angel.'

'The Whispering Angel.' Jack rolls the phrase around his mouth a couple of times. 'It's good! Thank you, boss.'

They sit on for half an hour or more. For some reason they are not tired. They don't speak much but appreciate the warm night air and watching the city sleep under the stars. The older man glances at his watch that says 3.42am.

'I should go home.'

'Me too.'

Together they take the lift down the Oxo Tower and exit by the main door onto Upper Ground where Jack heads for the Waterloo Tube and his boss turns the other way toward Southwark.

Young videographer

In a second-floor studio flat overlooking Cornwall Road, a young videographer is up very late. He is in his lounge playing about with the brand-new Panasonic Palmcorder video camera he has bought that afternoon. He makes his own little videos, his lofty aim one day to become a film director. Trying out the zooms and marvelling at the LCD viewfinder screen that allows for viewing, editing, or deleting, he is fiddling about with the lens to see what it is capable of.

It's just a camera for fun, not for serious film work, but a great little piece to use on holidays and to carry about with ease. Turning it to low-light conditions he takes it to the open window and focuses on the stars that are particularly luminous tonight. As he pans away in a slow arc down to the street below, on the other side of the road the young man notices a female with long blonde hair in a shiny black PVC mackintosh belted tightly at the waist. She is wearing glasses and black stockings and low black heels and seems very out of place on this quiet street.

On her way to hang around Waterloo Station, he presumes. Prossie looking for punters, no doubt. Carrying a shopping bag, seems oddly incongruous. What sort of a get-up is that for a warm night? She must be mad.

Something in the back of his brain tells him something is wrong but he can't think what. He supposes the black mac is to attract attention. Probably has nothing on underneath. She is closing the gap with a young man who is strolling ahead of her.

The videographer still has the feeling that this is more than just unusual and that he has somewhere seen or heard of this scene before. He just cannot work out where the strange sensation in his mind is coming from. Is this déjà vu? Not quite.

Has he seen these two before? He doesn't think so. He just cannot work it out. His camera follows the tart from the moment that she calls softly to the young man in front of her who stops and turns. Then she wiggles seductively up to him, pushes her face close to his and says something. Putting down the shopping bag, she shows him a piece of paper but drops it by mistake. The young man bends to pick it up. Before the cameraman knows it, the woman has slipped something over the man's head, thrown herself like an animal onto his back and is pulling his head back as hard as she can.

Horrified, the cameraman almost drops his camera but hanging onto it, hastily backs into his room. Unable to believe what he has just witnessed he stops and stands staring at the camera for a moment. Then he tiptoes back to the window and for some reason, pulls the blind down as quietly as he can, perhaps for fear he will be spotted.

That done, he slowly peeks around the side of it to see a much more shocking sight. Now, on the pavement, blood oozing from the body, the woman is crouched over it and doing something awful to it. He wants to but doesn't dare film any more. She might see him.

Then he realises what the feeling had been. Of course! He's read about the black PVC fibres. It is The Keeper! Shocked, he is shaking as he lifts the receiver from the telephone on the table by the door. He dials 999.

A woman replies. Speaking in a low voice for fear he might be overheard, he gives his name and address then loses patience and yells, 'The police need to come *now*! It's The Keeper! *At once!* Do you understand? The Keeper – the serial killer is killing a man right now on the street where I live!'

'Calm down please, sir. Could you please repeat your details for me? I am contacting the police directly but I need you to remain calm...'

CHAPTER THIRTY-SEVEN

It had been so hard holding myself back and far too long since Rob. Getting on for four months. So inhibiting waiting. But I had to in order to see what happened with that Rossi fellow, so I didn't go out at night until they let him go.

I wasn't sure how I would handle it if they found him guilty. I didn't want some dumb chap getting credit for my work that is done with such careful planning and skilful execution. There's only one Keeper, that's for sure. The stress was really getting to me and I was so relieved to be out on the streets again. I had to make myself wait a bit longer since they let Rossi go to give the boys in blue time to relax their guard and make them think no more murders were going to take place.

It was so good just to smell the night air and to know what was to happen. And then this young boy with curls turned a corner and walked into my life. He had the word 'next' emblazoned right across his sweet young body. He looked harmless enough but he needed taking care of. He could become a problem later in life. And he was so slight – so easy to manage.

He walked straight toward me and I turned the other way.

The place was not right. But Mother Fate had drawn us together. There could be no doubt. He had to be next.

I waited a heartbeat or two then turned again and followed as he walked until we reached a quiet street, then I went through the usual routine.

His face was slim with dark eyelashes framing dark-blue eyes and full lips. I could smell alcohol on his last breath.

I literally buzzed with pleasure as he expired. One less young man to worry about.

I left this one very late tonight and dawn was already up by the time I got home. It was too late. Note to self: what would Mamma say? Be more careful next time.

CHAPTER THIRTY-EIGHT

DR EDWARD FLYNN, FORENSIC PATHOLOGIST

'Dr Flynn, good morning, sir. I'm sorry to trouble you at this hour but a murder has been committed on the pavement of Cornwall Road, near Waterloo, SE1. The SOCO is already there, sir. I was told to inform you that it seems to be another of the same again.'

Edward looks at his watch and yawns. It is 0547. 'The same again, what do you mean? Oh, the serial killer. Oh dear, oh dear, I see. Understood. Thank you. Tell the SOCO I shall attend as quick as I can. Thank you, officer.'

A detective from Pollitt's team is already at the temporarily floodlit scene of the crime when Dr Flynn arrives. He introduces himself and brings the pathologist up to date about what has been reported by the young man in the flat opposite.

'A woman? In a black raincoat! So it really is a woman then. We wondered.'

'What is more, the killer and victim were also filmed by the young man with a camcorder from his window.'

'Filmed? Good Heavens! Whatever was he doing filming at such an hour?' Dr Flynn thought about it for a moment then said, 'Of course, this is very good news. At last, we know who we are looking for. Did he get a decent shot of her face, do you know? I should very much like to see that film, if I may?'

'At the moment, the cassette is at the station. Later in the morning it will be linked up to a special cassette player so we can view it on a TV. You'd be most welcome to drop in and take a look at it tomorrow if you'd like, Dr Flynn.'

'I am as keen as all of you to help find this killer. I have dealt with every one of the homicides, bar the first, and feel very involved with the deaths of these young men. Yes, thank you, I'd be interested to see this heinous female at work.'

The pathologist kneels by the corpse. Once again, he finds a few black fibres on the shirt and trousers Jack has been wearing. Once again, the victim has been garrotted with the same type of cord as before and once again, the genitals have been deftly removed. But this time, as with Rob, there is a two-inch-high initial P carved at the top of a thigh and after it a small x.

CHAPTER THIRTY-NINE

DI JO POLLITT

On night duty last night, Cilla has asked a nurse to take over early from her so that she can get back by 5.30am and we set off soon afterwards in order to beat the worst of the traffic. There's always a large amount heading west on the M3 and A303 on a Saturday in August but starting as early as we do we beat the worst of it.

Apart from the hotel booking, we've made no other plans. We both simply want to stop and allow life to go slow for a while.

We intend to walk along the coastal path at our leisure – nothing too hearty, more of a meander but we shall cover some ground.

We'll do a short walk for about an hour or so this afternoon just to see the coast and feel the sand between our toes. We've been down this way before but not to this stretch of the coastal path. We usually try different areas and have had some great times in Cornwall. We have fantasised about one day when we retire of buying a house together down there and getting a dog to walk with us.

A recharge is needed, especially for me with all the stress I have been through. Cilla, who works hard too, is only too happy to take the brakes off for a while. All we both want is to get some much-needed sleep, to read – me my historical biographies, Cilla her crime novels of which she cannot get enough – to be fed nice meals and to walk and swim in the sea as and when we feel like it.

We travel in the Golf. It's reliable, trustworthy and solid – bit like Smith, I suppose. I take the first part of the drive while Cilla falls asleep after a busy night at the surgery and I am irritated when my mobile rings at o61o. I scrabble about trying to find the phone in my bag.

'Jo, leave it!' Woken by the sound, Cilla is quite snappy. 'The M3 is dangerous enough without you jabbering on the phone while driving. You're on hols, remember? It's nothing that can't wait. It can only be the Met this early. You're taking time out, remember? Forget that wretched thing.'

Cilla grabs the bag from me as the mobile continues to ring and she fumbles about until she finds it and switches it off. 'There, it's off. I know I'm an interfering bossy-boots but someone has to look after you. We all managed fine without them only a year ago. Promise me you won't use it again this holiday. You're exhausted and you need to let go of all the stresses in this world for just a week.'

I put my palm on my friend's thigh and give it a friendly squeeze. 'Thanks, Cilla. You're absolutely right. Everything you say makes sense. I'll leave the thing off. I just can't help being twitchy in case it's work.'

'Well, if it is, they've no right to call you. You're on leave. Now, let's just forget about blooming Southwark Police and enjoy our holiday, huh?'

I grin. Sometimes I don't know what I'd do without Cilla.

We hit a fair amount of traffic on the way down which gets worse when we get onto the A303. We pass Stonehenge over to our right sometime around 0830. The iconic stone circle is lit by the morning sun beaming to ensure the break starts well.

I am to share the driving with Cilla so pull in to a lay-by here where we stop. Cilla wakes up and I get out the thermos flask and two mugs from the picnic bag. We glug some coffee and munch on some custard creams while gazing at the distant prehistoric site that never fails to give cause for wonder.

We have planned to get to our hotel in time to check in, go for a wander, then find somewhere for lunch.

Cilla takes over the wheel and when we begin to curl round the north edge of Dartmoor we get glimpses of the far distant moorland and start to feel we are properly in the West Country, both sharing our excitement to be here. We cut across the land from Okehampton in Devon to north Cornwall to reach our hotel by about 1100.

The Ship is on the coast in Bude, an old and romantic coastal town surrounded by sandstone cliffs. It was once a Victorian bathing resort and boasts a harbour and a castle. We check in then go for a stroll until we find a small café where we sit sunning ourselves outside and have more coffees but with cake this time.

We sit happily watching the sea rolling in and afterwards potter off for our first walk of the holiday where we climb up an easy cliff to a Victorian tower called Compass Point.

Up here it's grassy but windy, totally worth it for the magnificent views. We can see as far as Tintagel as the Atlantic surges into the coastline below us. We lie down on our tummies side by side looking out to sea and say nothing. After a time I glance at Cilla and notice tears running down her cheeks. I am so surprised.

'Hey, whatever is it, Cill? Whatever's wrong?'

'Sorry,' she says, 'I'm really sorry. It's nothing. It just creeps up on me sometimes. It's just about something that happened ages ago and occasionally the memory hits me and upsets me. Sorry Jo, I'll stop now. Forget it ever happened.'

She is desperately wiping at her eyes in an attempt to stem the tears but they keep on coming.

Whatever this is, it is something deeply serious. Not prone to weeping or hysteria of any kind, Cilla is a tough girl who can withstand knocks. I am shaken and worried.

'You can tell *me*, you know you can. If you've been bottling this up for a long time, it sounds like its time it should be released and what better place? On top of a cliff with only you, me and the ocean to listen?'

She shakes her head. 'I can't, I just can't. It's too difficult to talk about.' She is now sobbing her heart out.

I take hold of her nearest hand. 'But you can if you want to. The lid on your kettle is ready to fly off, darling. Remember a problem shared is a problem...' I catch myself and stop. Enough with the clichés. After a pause I say, 'Look, if you want to talk about it, now's probably the best time you'll ever have, but I am not going to try to push you into it. Just know that whatever it is, I will neither judge nor disapprove nor take any stance whatsoever. The only thing I shall ever try to do is to help you, Cilla. I adore you. Always will and always have. That's all.'

And this is when the floodgates open. She tells me she was raped when she was fifteen. She spares no details as she wails and howls her pain and misery to the wind and sea.

Shocked to the core, I don't know what to say. But I know how I feel and rage burns inside me. Now I know why she and her family moved to Kennington when she was sixteen. To get away from the place where she'd been attacked.

When I get time, I shall dig meticulously through old police files and try my hardest to see whether I may be able to match the rapist with other later rapes. If I can get just a little vengeance for Cilla, I shall do so, and that, I promise myself, is a promise.

We share a large twin room in the hotel. We've been on holiday together for years but are shy about dressing and undressing in front of one another and always take our clothes to the bathroom to do this independently.

On the Sunday morning before we go down for breakfast, already showered and dressed, I sneak a look at my phone while Cilla is having a shower. I see the number that rung is Tony Smith's mobile which I now know pretty well by heart. I quietly pocket the mobile and knock on the shower door. Cilla turns off the water and peers through the slightly open door. I can't help seeing her pretty body as I say, 'Sorry to interrupt but I'm going to nip down and take a stroll round the gardens. I feel like a bit of Cornish air. See you in the restaurant at 9am. Okay?'

When I get downstairs, I slip through a side door into the large, grand garden with its vast, sweeping lawn. Beyond, the sea gleams in the sunshine and I take a deep breath. I am joyful, a feeling I had forgotten existed. This is such a beautiful place. The garden has a flight of enticing stone steps that lead down to the edge of the cliff above the inviting green sea. A well-placed bench begs me to sit and wonder at the view.

I park myself on the seat and take the mobile from my pocket. The heavy little thing has already become a habit in the few months I've had it and I am discovering the feeling of wondering how any of us ever managed before they existed. I glance over my shoulder towards the hotel feeling guilty that I am breaking my word to Cilla. Worse, I know my pal is right.

But even though it's a Sunday and he is likely to be at home I can't resist calling Tony.

He answers almost immediately. 'Howdeedo!' Then corrects himself quickly when he hears who it is. 'Oh scuse me, hello ma'am, wasn't expecting you. Hope you're having a good time?'

'Yes lovely, thank you. Just wondered why you rang yesterday?'

'Oh yes, ma'am, well I wasn't sure whether I should call or not but decided you'd never forgive me if I didn't. I just felt I had to tell you. Don't quite know how to say it but, it's happened again.'

'What? What has?'

'Another killing.'

'God! Oh no! Oh hell! Where? When? God! I'll come back.'

'Yesterday morning, early hours. Usual MO, found in a street between Southwark and Waterloo. He's back to where he started except that he has turned out to be a she! And again she's carved the letter P and another x into the body. Who knows what it means but there's no doubt it's another message.'

'A woman! Jesus Henry Christ! Delaney always said it was possible. Right. I'll come back tomorrow if you can hold the fort until Tuesday?'

'No, you're not to. The super says you're to have the holiday. He's on it himself. I think he wants to do this, ma'am. He's missed being on cases. Now's his opportunity. His back already seems surprisingly better. We're coping. We can manage. I just had to let you know because it'll be in the papers and on the news. The amazing thing is that somebody filmed her.'

Tony explains about the videographer and that the film, dark though it was, shows enough footage just to make out the murderess and her pitiful victim.

'Tell him to call Delaney.'

'Super wouldn't hear of it, ma'am. Actually he's already blaming him for being wrong.'

'Huh! We all thought it was Rossi. The super as much as any of us. And he was the last one to contemplate a female.'

'I know. But you know what he's like.'

'Indeed I do, Tony. I have to think about this. I have brought a friend with me and it's her holiday too. Naturally, my instinct is to drive back today, but I must consider her. Let me think about it. It's a tricky one.'

I stare at the sea that now seems cold, grey and forbidding. 'I just can't believe this has happened. We were so sure it was...'

I start to cry. This is not something I ever do. Desperate to hide the sound of my tears from Tony, I manage 'Speak soon,' and click off the phone. My hand has been clutching the receiver so hard, my knuckles feel stiff and I notice they have gone white.

I sit looking out to sea. What can I do? I have broken my word to Cilla. Another young man has lost his life. And now, to make matters worse, Maurie is trying to take over from me. It's my case, not his.

I am in despair as I try to find a way to deal with what has happened. How can I tell Cilla? I don't care too much about the lost money on the week, although it's a wretched shame and I have really been looking forward to this. But the killer comes first. This is the biggest case of my life and there is not likely to be another as big again. At least, I hope not. My pride in my work is vital to me. I close my eyes and feel Mum's hand rest on my shoulders.

'What's up?'

I jump as I realise it is Cilla behind me. My friend crosses in front of me and sits next to me. She sees the mobile still clutched in my hand.

'What is it, Jo? You look as white as a sheet.'

'No really, I'm fine. I think it's just exhaustion. Now that I can relax, I feel shattered.'

'What's with the phone?'

'Oh, I was just checking who called. It was the neighbour just telling me the cats are fine! She's such a silly woman, but she's feeding them so what can I do?'

'Ask her not to call unless it's an emergency.'

But I can tell Cilla doesn't believe a word I've just said. She can see how shocked I am feeling. She sighs and says she wishes we could just have some time to ourselves where my job didn't interfere. But she decides to leave it for now and allow whatever has happened to sink into my mind. She will tackle the subject later. All she wants is for us both to have a rest and to have a bit of 'us' time. She seems so happy to have got that huge burden of pain off her chest yesterday.

'Come on, breakfast stops being served in five minutes. We'd better run.'

We do that and get back to the hotel dining room just in time to order some food and tea for Cilla, coffee for me.

Cilla expects me to go for the full English as I usually do while she herself will plump for the cereal followed by the kippers and toast. But I've gone quiet. I have become so distracted and off-colour that I absent-mindedly asked for croissants and tea.

Cilla stops the waitress and says, 'Sorry, but can you make that coffee, please? My friend is not a tea drinker at breakfast.'

When the breakfast arrives, Cilla tries to lighten the atmosphere by gently pointing out the elderly, unspeaking couple across the room. He with a laughable, dyed comb-over that just doesn't work and she, spectacles as thick as milk bottle bottoms.

That fails so she mentions the beauty of the place and asks what I might have in mind for today. I am so shocked all I can do is gaze at the croissants and jams and leave my coffee untouched.

Finally, Cilla has had enough. 'Right, Jo. You have to tell me what it is that you have just learned. Yesterday I shared my deepest, most difficult secret ever with you and you have to tell me what is going on. I refuse to spend a week with you if you are going to be like this. I have only seen you this distraught after your mum died. What is it? What has happened? Tell me or I leave right now.'

This jerks me out of my reverie. I look long and hard at my dearest friend. 'I don't know how to tell you.'

'Tell me what?'

I look out of the window. I look around the room. I look anywhere but at Cilla.

'Tell me what?'

'There's been another murder.'

'Oh no! Oh good God! There can't have been. I don't believe it!'

'I didn't... but it's true.'

Cilla sits back in her chair. She digests the news. She looks disconsolately out of the window. 'Let's finish breakfast then go outside again and talk about it.'

She butters some croissants, puts honey on them and is now feeding them to me. She pours me a large cup of coffee and hands it to me. 'Drink it. It'll help.'

Relief floods over me. My friend is looking after me once more, as she did when Mum died. My inner voice has a word in my ear. *And at the same time you can tell her how much you need her and how deeply you really feel about her and perhaps take her into your arms...* But I say nothing.

When that is done, we leave the dining room and return to the bench at the end of the garden where we sat before in front of that wonderful view. We talk and talk and talk and are more open than we had ever been before.

Now that she has revealed the terrible thing that happened to her, I feel I can tell her anything at all. I fill her in with all the details Smith has told me which she is fascinated by, in particular the fact that it's a woman who was filmed. I don't feel I can ask her to go home straight away. That would be going too far.

My emotions churn and behind them Rossi's face regards me with fear. Deep down I know I will never be free of this image and the guilt of treating an innocent man so badly.

The one thing that makes me wish I was back in London there and then is the fact that the murder has been filmed. I want personally to interview the young videographer and to see that thing called a miniDV soon as. Apparently, it's the latest kind of videotape and is set to become all the rage.

In the end, it is agreed that we will cut the holiday short and get back to London late on Tuesday evening. I will be back in the office by Wednesday morning. It is also agreed that I will call Maurie on Monday morning and tell him I am back on the case as the senior investigating officer. I'm not going to have him taking over from me now. There's no doubt the reason he's been so eager is on account of the film. They have evidence of what he – I have to correct myself – she looks like.

This will make all the difference to the hunt. If the super tries to take over from me, I will kick up and make such a stink. He was a great detective in his day but I doubt he will ever work out who the killer is.

A new corner has been turned in our relationship. Cilla and I have both revealed more of our feelings than ever before. In the afternoon we stroll along the coastal path, barely noticing the many others we meet on the way, so engrossed are we in our conversation.

I tell Cilla I love her, in the truest, deepest, most meaningful sense of the word and with huge relief Cilla stops and turns to face me. I stop too. She puts her hands on my arms and says it is completely reciprocated and that she has always loved me like that too.

We both feel a little awkward and are not sure how to go forward, so we link arms and walk slowly on in silence toward the distant horizon where the sun paints the water in colours and we absorb the enormity of what has been said.

It is Cilla who stops again, turns to face me, tilts her head slightly back and to one side and invites me to kiss her. Tentative at first, our barely touching lips soon grow bolder. Once we have taken the leap, our mutual feelings so long repressed, now explode into sensual expression.

We are both completely surprised by the strength of the passion that takes us over. As we walk back to the hotel, we both feel awkward with our strange new situation. A barrier has been lifted and there is no going back. I think we each feel scared in our separate ways.

In the end, I murmur, 'We're bound to feel strange. And we can both back out of this now, if we want. I don't want to. But if you have any doubt at all, you must say.'

Cilla pokes me hard in the ribs. 'Oh, stop being so dramatic, Pollitt! We love each other and of course it's going to feel funny for a bit but that's okay. We must lap up every second of how we feel. This is what they call "being in love" and apparently, it's supposed to make you feel a bit crazy. Mind you, I've been in love with you for years.'

'And I've been in love with you for years...' We cackle, giggle, laugh, hug and kiss, then run back to the hotel to get down a celebration cocktail or three at the bar.

Our mutual declaration is nervously consummated this night and we are left amazed, thrilled and slightly bemused by what our bodies are capable of doing and feeling. Once again for me, little sleep is had but this time for the best possible reasons.

Marco Rossi

In the mess that the police left his flat, which Marco has done his best to restore to some semblance of what it was, he sits on the ripped couch watching the Sunday evening news on the television.

He can hardly believe his eyes and ears when the newscaster announces that the serial killer known as 'The Keeper' has killed again and that now the police are certain it is a woman. She was filmed by someone who happened to be at their window with their video camera while she was attacking her victim, a young male named Jack Wilson. He was walking home after a late shift at the Oxo Tower restaurant where he worked as an assistant sommelier.

Rossi jumps up from the sofa and runs on the spot for a second while he claps his hands. This is elation due to pure relief. At last his name will be cleared. At last that lone journalist who is still trailing him will stop following him and at last, he can expect a full and proper apology from the Southwark Police.

He only remembers to feel sad for the victim when he goes into the kitchen to crack open a bottle of Chianti to celebrate his moment.

DI Jo Pollitt

The only thing that gets in the way of my new happiness is the guilt I hold over our – and in particular my – bad treatment of Rossi.

I berate myself for falling under Delaney's spell by allowing myself to be persuaded that he was right about Rossi. Of course, I know why I did so. Results, results, results. Please the Home Secretary, please the Commissioner for the Metropolitan Police, please the super; the press; the public; please every effing one, including myself.

But that old superego inner voice or whatever it is, is unhappy with me and I feel an aching self-reproach for the unnecessary pain and anxiety that unfortunate man suffered. I must really press on Maurie to offer the poor bloke a full apology and to pay for any repairs needed following our searches of his flat.

On the way back to London, Cilla and I talk about our future together. We agree that I need to lay the ghosts of the house I live in and that a move would help me to progress forward from my mum's death.

Cilla's place is a rented single-bed flat near her place of work at Elephant and Castle and too small for us, as we need an extra room for exercising et cetera; besides, with the money I should raise from selling the house in Kennington, with Cilla helping pay towards a mortgage there would be enough to buy us a two-bed place convenient for Southwark and Cilla's veterinary surgery.

We discuss whereabouts we'd like to live and other exciting plans about how we can at last properly share our lives. We dream that when we retire it will be to a cottage down here where we both feel happier than we can believe. The only sadness for both of us that I cannot tell Mum and that Cilla is going to find it difficult to tell her parents, as they are about as strait-laced as they come.

But, I say, she doesn't need to come out to them. Just tell them we're sharing on practical grounds as old friends. They never need know, if she can't face telling them. But, she says, she will. She wants to and if they're silly about it, it's their loss.

We decide that straight away Cilla will hand in her notice to her landlady who will require three months' notice as it is a long-term unfurnished rental and that before that she will gradually move stuff over to my place and move in with me. I am so thrilled about this I feel like a forty-two-year-old teenager in love. Judging from the glow she is giving off I think my lover does too.

CHAPTER FORTY

DCS MAURICE GREEN

Maurice Green finishes his dinner. The wife has made a bloody marvellous paella and he is full to bursting, having had two portions. Unusually, he hadn't been able to manage a dessert.

Mind you, the weather is not conducive to large amounts of food as the heat has built up over London over the past week and the place is humid as anything. It makes people sleepy and heavy-headed and it's hard to think straight. Everyone is struggling in these conditions and waiting in hope that a large thunderstorm will break over the city to alleviate the repressive heat.

Maurice is not dreading tomorrow in the way he dreaded today last night. As soon as he heard about the film of the woman killer, he grabbed at the idea of placing himself in charge of the serial killer case in Jo's absence. A miniDV camcorder was ordered in, but in spite of the technicians playing around with the gamma to enhance the woman's face, it has been impossible to really see her and the film is little help apart from capturing the gender of the killer.

With her head turned away from the camera, all that can be seen in the darkness is that the woman has long blonde hair and that she is wearing glasses. The team has run through as many possible female suspects as they can find on their books, coming up with just one who, it had turned out, was serving a long term in Holloway prison. So they are back to square one.

And what the hell that 'P' stood for, God only knew. If it was supposed to be a clue to help them find this madwoman, it failed. It is presumed to be her signature and that her name begins with a P. Patricia, Pamela, Peggy, Polly... it is no help at all. Just a tease. P for Pollitt is the most likely as the detective in charge of the case.

Thank goodness, he thinks, that he is going to be able to hand it back to her with no loss of face. And she wants it, and what is more, he will come out of it looking like he has done the right thing by stepping into the breach at the vital moment.

He knows deep down that in the new circumstances Jo will make a better job of it than he. After all, he reasons, it takes a woman to know a woman.

DI Jo Pollitt

I am in my office by just before 8am on Wednesday morning. I have already spoken to Maurie on the phone. Once he realised the difficulties involved in engaging himself back on the ground in the workforce as the leader of my team, he accepted my return with more alacrity than I expected.

The first thing I do is to watch the miniDV a number of times. I stop and start it, run it backwards and forwards, slow it down, but however hard I try, I cannot see the woman's face. The light is too low. One can see her hair and the mac and although the cameraman has done his best to get a close-up of the woman, the lighting conditions and the angle just didn't make it possible.

The murder, though, is plain to see.

The next thing I arrange is to visit the young videographer at his office, which is in Soho. After a long discussion with him, I thank and praise him for being a model citizen and assure him that two new film cassettes and a reward of £20 are being sent round to him this afternoon by way of gratitude and compensation for his trouble.

I then pay a visit to Dr Flynn who is at the mortuary dealing with another death. We discuss the extraordinary fact that the serial killer is female.

Unfortunately, he has nothing new to offer in the way of evidence found on the body of this latest wretched victim. He has puzzled and puzzled over the letter P and eventually decided he believes it is the killer's signature.

'Would it be worth checking through police records to find any female who has attacked a man before whose first name or possibly surname starts with that letter?'

'I'll give it a go. Thanks for the idea, Edward.' I don't want to squash the man by telling him we've already tried that tack with no luck.

On the way back to the station, I have an idea. When I get there, I call Tony to come into my office. 'It has occurred to me to get a sniffer dog on her trail.'

'Bow wow, ma'am! What a great idea.'

'Not bad, is it? She'll have the blood on her mac and probably a spatter or more on her shoes. I reckon a highly trained dog – bloodhound or spaniel – could track her trail. Not sure we still use bloodhounds anymore, do we?'

'I think we stopped using them years ago in favour of more all-rounder dogs like German Shepherds. Bloodhounds are single-minded, I believe.'

'It'd be great for this use though. Can you get on to the dog unit and find out soon as? We need a champion blood-sniffer.'

Tony does not take long. He comes back with the news that a police dog unit has a sniffer dog in the shape of a springer spaniel called Pickles that is exceptional with cadavers and blood scents and that along with its handler will be only too happy to help. They are standing – or sitting – by, as the case may be in Lewisham now awaiting their command from the inspector.

A thrill of positivity runs through me as I arrange for the street to be cordoned off again this afternoon. The scene of crime is still taped off with a policeman guarding it. Tony has already arranged for the policewoman to bring her dog up to Southwark and they are now ready to accompany us to the crime scene.

Driven by Tony, me, a PC, the dog handler and brown-and-white springer spaniel Pickles arrive in Cornwall Road at 3.56pm.

Pickles' tail seems to be wired to permanently wag. A dog who charms us all with her excellent manners, smiling face and positive nature, she is led to the scene of the crime. Here, the rate of wag goes into top gear and excitement overtakes the bitch who barks in ecstasy when she sniffs the pavement where the murder has taken place.

Her handler says something to her dog that no one understands but that sets the dog racing down the road, nose glued to the pavement, tail going like the clappers. Her handler clings to the end of the lead running to keep up with her.

Now there are four people chasing after the dog. A pair of women in one of the flats in the road see us passing and watch out of their window in complete amazement, giggling at the strange sight.

Pickles takes us to the end of the road, around a corner, down another short street and finally to another lane where she runs a bit further and suddenly jerks to a halt.

She stands wagging and barking and jumping at a black-lidded rubbish bin. Tony removes the lid. The spaniel jumps up and sniffs at the interior of the bin in a very excited manner, barking furiously. The bin is empty.

'Er, what do you think?'

'I reckon your villain put something with blood on it in here.'

The dog handler encourages Pickles to come away and try sniffing the pavement beyond to see if she could pick up the trail again, but the dog seems to find nothing except whatever had been in the bin. We are all out of breath and sweating with the humidity.

'I reckon the knife must have been chucked in here,' I say. 'I'll send some guys up tomorrow for a proper search again. Brilliant dog, Pickles.' I pat the dog's head, tickle her ears and know that one day Cilla and I will have a dog of our own.

Cilla, the great lover of animals, has always said that once she retired, she couldn't wait to get a dog. Now, it will be ours – or perhaps we will have one each. I almost smile at the thought but manage to bring myself back from my flight of fancy. This is happening to me quite a lot at the moment. This heady new experience of reciprocated love fills my head and I have to keep pulling myself back from thinking about my beloved new lover. It feels quite odd that I am living through such a wondrous thing at my age. But I'm not about to question it.

'What a shame the bins have been emptied. It so nearly worked. We'll requisition this one and get it checked by forensics.' I shake the dog handler's hand. 'Thank you so much and of course, Pickles. Wish I had a tit-bit to give her.'

'Don't worry ma'am, I come ready provided with tit-bits.'

I continue, 'Let me see, Southwark Council, same as us – what day are our bins collected, any idea, Tony?'

''Fraid not, ma'am.'

'Constable?'

'Sorry, ma'am.'

I call the station and speak to the sergeant on call duty. He knows. 'Tuesdays, Ma'am.'

'Would you believe? Tuesdays. Right. So, the council refuse collection department phone number...' I am more or less talking to myself now while I dial 192 and get directory enquiries who give me the number.

I turn to the constable. 'Please stay with it now, constable, and we'll send a van with some notices for you to leave on doors of likely owners of the bin to tell them we need it as evidence in a police enquiry. And then the van will bring you and the bin back to get it to forensics.'

The others climb back into Tony's Fiesta, Pickles panting in the back.

'To the station please, Tony. I'll call the council on the way. Once we can trace where the rubbish was taken, we'll need the wonderful Pickles again. She'll find what we want. Let's get back to the station.'

'Er, excuse me just a moment, Inspector Pollitt.' From the back seat the dog-handler taps me on the shoulder. 'Pickles will need something of the same scent she followed today to know what she's looking for or we could pick up all sorts of false leads.'

'Ah, so what do you suggest?'

'Well, we don't have a piece of cloth or anything convenient like that, but we do have the bin. Better bring that with us.' She laughs but is deadly serious. 'And we have another couple of dogs we could bring too. For a job like this, the more dogs, the better. I'll bring my colleague and his two dogs with me if that's okay, inspector?'

'Quite right. As you say, the more the better.'

I ring the council and discover that the landfill site is in Rainham in Essex. Since the bin has been collected by a certain refuse collection vehicle, as they are nowadays called, the waste collection people can trace the driver and arrange for him to accompany the police along with the dogs and their handlers to the tip the following morning.

CHAPTER FORTY-ONE

DI JO POLLITT

A torrential storm broke overnight and I for one had a bad evening. Thunder cracked and banged for some time while the lightning was so violent, bright and frequent that it quite scared those of us who watched it from our windows.

By morning, the storm has ended, thank God, so our pending trip to Essex won't be a sodden one. The driver of the waste collection vehicle is called Sam. He obligingly arrives at the police station at 9am. I don't need to go and could easily send one of my detectives but I am so invested in this hunt that I'm not going to miss a thing.

Pickles and her handler, along with two others with one German Shepherd and one more spaniel are waiting patiently too. This time they are in a large van that can contain them all, including the bin, which sends Pickles mad with excitement. Her handler quietens her and they drive across a still warm but now tolerable London. They cross the river by Southwark Bridge and drive all the way to Rainham Marshes where the landfill site is to be found.

Vast mountains of wet, stinking rubbish greet us and all of us are shocked by the sheer height of the man-made hills as well as the quantity of stuff that appears to stretch away for ever. The stench is overwhelming and unlike the quiet wasteland I expected, there is traffic, noise and vermin everywhere.

Sam directs us to the exact area where he tipped his lorry on Tuesday afternoon. Other lorries have since emptied over and around the place and I curse under my breath. 'How are we ever going to find what we're looking for?'

I feel a hand on my arm.

'These are pretty amazing dogs, inspector. You'll be surprised what they can do. They can dig, too. Let's give them their leads and see what happens.'

I am grateful to this good-natured, helpful dog-handler.

Pickles and the other dogs are wearing paw protection dog boots that they have been trained to wear when digging in hazardous areas. They look quite comic. They are shown the bin to sniff and their handlers say something incomprehensible that the dogs understand at once. Set free and directed to the area of waste Sam has shown them, they scoot this way and that way, sideways, up and down the vast hill of garbage while we stand watching and holding anything we can find over our faces. The heat doesn't help the repellent stink. The dogs sniff and wag about on the side of the hill in front of them.

'However can they distinguish the one smell from all these others?' asks Tony.

One of the handlers answers, 'Certain breeds of dogs have better senses of smell than others. Apparently, these particular dogs have between 225 and 300 million smell receptors in their noses, as compared to just five million in a human nose. Amazing, isn't it?'

'Amazing,' Tony and I say in unison.

I tell myself to remember this incredible information. Where previously I would have to remind myself to mention my surprise in the evening's phone call to Cilla, who of course will know such a thing, I can now simply tell her when I get home. The thought washes a delicious sensation of calm over me. I am just getting used to being happily in love. It's a lovely feeling.

After sniffing about for some long time, one of the spaniels stops and begins digging. Everything from empty packets to plastic and glass bottles to broken bits and pieces, tins of all kinds, a number of old shoes, a broken tennis racket fly through the air and hurtle down the hill as the surprisingly strong dog flings them out of his way. He digs with a frantic determination and as he burrows deeper his tail wags faster. After a while longer, the tail takes on a circular motion, almost too fast to see.

His handler clambers up the waste hill as the dog's head followed by half his body disappears into the hole. Finally the animal emerges, clutching a filthy-looking piece of something in its mouth. The handler takes the offensive-looking article from the dog to find it is a plastic glove. She rewards the dog with a tit-bit. Meanwhile the other dogs keep sniffing and digging. Close by to the glove find, Pickles surfaces from the tip with a piece of dirty crushed plastic between her teeth.

'Come, come.'

The dogs run down the stinking hill after the handlers. When they reach the group, told to drop, Pickles deposits the mangled something she is carrying in front of them. Her handler gives her a tit-bit too. Tony, who has come armed with latex gloves, picks it up, pulls and shakes the crushed plastic out until it begins to form a flattened shape and becomes recognisable. It is a dirty, black, blood-spattered PVC mackintosh. With a drawstring hood, it is long enough to cover a tall person's knees.

The glove and the raincoat are taken straight to forensics. Dr Flynn insists on personally testing them and they are proved to have Jack's blood on them. There is some DNA on them as well. Infuriatingly, after a long search through the database, no match can be found. This is little help to me and my team but what we do now have is a label inside the mackintosh that reads *AVE 100% waterproof.*

Studying the crowded whiteboard at the station, I draw heavily on a Camel, my new lover nagging my mind about how much I am smoking these days and how bad it is for me. I have promised her I'll do my best to give up once we've caught this evil woman.

I scan the latest photographs. Five murders. The press serve it up almost daily. Londoners are frightened, especially young men. At least now they know it is a woman who wears black plastic macs, so any young man out on the streets late at night will run a mile if they see her. Although now she will change what she wears as it has been widely publicised.

So far, we haven't been able to trace where she bought the raincoats. The one we have appears to be a generic type that campers and festival-goers use. They come ready packed in a plastic envelope and weigh nothing, ideal to slip into a backpack. There's no size label which indicates they're sold as one size fits all. If there are any more murders (and why should there not be?) we shall have to alert the public and enlist their help to check their bins every morning before the bin men come.

My mobile rings. It is Delaney. 'Hi Jo. Miss me? Just wondered how you're getting along.'

'One, yes, I really do miss you, Patrick, and two, not well.'

'My newspapers tell me it's a woman.'

'Yes, you were right all along. You always said it could be.'

'Well, I'm not ringing to crow. Just to see how you are. Have you got any further evidence or clues?'

'Not a thing except we found a black PVC mac and a glove in landfill. Fat lot of good that's done us.'

'I could always meet you in secret, you know, just to talk it through with you. Green doesn't have to know. I only want to help, Jo.'

'That's so good of you, Patrick. How can I resist? Shall we meet at the Red Lion one day soon?'

'Today, if you like. I'm not busy. After work?'

'That would be great. I'd love to pick your clever brains.'

'Seven o'clock and let's grab some of their delectably tasteless frozen scampi in a basket while we're at it?'

'Scrummy, not. Yes, let's.'

Two things occur to me after I put down the phone. The first is that now Cilla is living with me, I should let her know I'll be home late and the second is that I forgot to mention the letter P and the x carved into the thigh. I'll tell Delaney later.

The Irish in his voice strikes me again.

'I'm still unclear about why she emasculates these young men. I fail to believe it can be to keep their genitals at home and fantasise over them. You're not going to like this, Jo, but there is a possibility that she cooks and eats them.'

'Oh God, Patrick. How disgusting!'

'Well, think of prairie oysters.'

My stomach heaves as I look at my scampi.

'Sorry. But you see, I've always been certain that if this is a female it is someone with a big hatred of males.'

'Then why choose young ones in particular? Surely if that were the case she needn't roam so far afield and could pick on any male.'

'The male who sparked this hatred has to have been the same sort of age. My thoughts are that she was abused either by an older sibling, cousin or someone between the ages of thirty and twenty.'

'Then why poor Winston?'

'Convenience. Practice. He appeared at the right time.'

'Do you think she may live in his neighbourhood then? Might she be black? And what do you think might have been the starting signal that pushed this woman into committing these murders?'

'One, possibly; two, possibly; three, it's usually an event that releases the pent-up rage. A life experience that incurs loss is the most common. A job, the death of someone close, anything major could set the spark that lights the fire.'

My scampi has quite lost its appeal. I take a long swig of my gin and tonic (no Cosmos here) and I want a cigarette but Delaney is eating, so I restrain myself. I feel as though Rossi is watching us. Being with Delaney brings back our mistake and guilt courses through me.

'Eat up, inspector. You need to keep your strength up.' He grins at me.

'Your earlier description has put me right off.' But that breaks the spell and, taking a mouthful of crunchy chips first dipped into tartare sauce, I manage to put the image out of my mind and munch the cotton-wool scampi.

We eat in silence for a few minutes then he says, 'They're all close to Northern line Tube stations. Did you realise that?'

'They are, it's true. Not sure how that helps us though.'

'Only in that she probably lives somewhere close to a stop along the line.'

'Probably.'

'Now it's in the news, she'll have to think up a different get-up. No way will she wear the black mac again. Far too recognisable.'

'What do you suppose she will do instead? She has her modus operandi perfectly worked out. She'll still want to wear a disposable plastic.'

'She will. I hate to say it but unless some miracle occurs and we find a decent lead, we shall have to wait and see.'

Silence follows. Each deep in our own thoughts.

'Anything else to tell me?'

'Oh yes, I forgot to tell you, once again the murderer carved the letter P with a small x beside it which we took to mean a kiss.'

'P? Really? And an x again. She's getting bolder by the minute, isn't she?'

'We are presuming it is a signature.'

'So her name could start with a P, you think.'

'That's what we thought at the station. Any ideas?'

'Unless it's a message to you, DI P for Pollitt.'

'Or for P for Patrick, come to that,' I retort, but then the killer couldn't possibly have known Delaney was working on the case, could she? Or could she? For a moment I wonder, then put the thought out of my mind.

Out of the blue I hear myself asking him, 'Ever been married, Patrick?'

'Can't say I have. Managed to avoid that obstacle so far. Whatever made you ask that, Jo?'

'Oh, I don't know, it just suddenly occurred to me.'

He looks at me, his head on one side, a wry smile on his face. God, I hope he doesn't think I fancy him. I shrug my shoulders and look away in a manner he will know to mean I don't.

We part company with a hug and promise to meet again before long.

The team is trying to trace the makers of the mackintosh and soon discover AVE is an American company that sells to a UK import company that offers various items including the disposable macs through newspaper and magazine columns and mail-order catalogues.

Our attempts to check where the killer had bought hers are fruitless. They are sold through so many outlets that the police have given up trying to trace where they have all been sold. They hoped to narrow it down to orders from people with London addresses but so many sellers have not kept records, it has eventually proved to be a fruitless task.

MONDAY SEPTEMBER 2ND TO
SEPTEMBER 25TH, 1996

CHAPTER FORTY-TWO

DCS MAURICE GREEN

The pain in Green's back has returned. It is playing him up badly now. The wife has bought him a special seat which helps when he sits down but the sciatica in his leg is getting worse. He is starting to rely more and more on painkillers.

These in turn make him sleepy and fog his brain. He is really struggling and, unheard of in the man's entire career, he has lately had to have a few days off work.

A visit to the doctor has not improved his humour when it has been suggested that he should try to lose some weight since that could be having a significant effect on his back. It is true, he accepts that he may have put on a few pounds or so in the last year. Others who know the once well-built man would have said to the contrary.

His desk job and his penchant for food and wine have added a large increase to the man's waist measurement and the weight has crept up slowly but surely, making a man who weighed thirteen stone now sixteen.

All Maurice wants is to get this bloody killer found. It has ruined his last year with the Met and he feels almost cheated that such a thing should have happened on his watch.

And worse than that, to add to his troubles, the Commissioner has been on to him. That is, the Commissioner of the Metropolitan Police, the head honcho himself.

There was a call.

'Superintendent Green, I have Sir Paul on the line. Are you able to take his call now?'

'Oh yes, please put him on.'

'Superintendent Green, good morning. Just a quick call to find out how things are going in the hunt for the serial killer of young men? Sadly, there appears to be some real fear around on the streets of our capital and we really do need to catch this weird female killer. Now, if it's a matter of resources or manpower, I can definitely help there. But if it's a matter of strategy, then I think we need to put our heads together over this one. I'd like to hear your views on this, superintendent. We've really got to pull out all the stops to catch this woman, haven't we? I mean, it's not reflecting well on the Met at all. Especially since it has turned out to be a woman. It somehow makes us look ridiculous that we are consistently outwitted by a female. What do you say, superintendent?'

Maurice stammers as he replies... 'W-well, sir, I've– I've been co-contemplating removing the detective inspector in charge of the case and giving it to another. We have even employed a criminal profiler to help us but so far no luck. This murderer is a remarkably clever person who leaves no trace of herself at all. A very rare and extremely hard case to crack, sir... but we are getting closer.'

Maurie explains how the sniffer dogs helped and about the video of the killer and after a long discussion, the Commissioner agrees to give it one more month before he gives the case to Scotland Yard.

DI Jo Pollitt

What has happened in my relationship with Cilla is making

a huge difference to the way I feel about my job. Now, whatever happens, however grim things become in the force, however many disappointments and failures I have to face, I have Cilla to love, Cilla to care for, but best of all, Cilla to come home to.

The only nights she's not there are when she sleeps in the surgery. My inner voice has little to say these days and I don't even notice its absence. Whenever we have a day off, together we visit estate agents and think about putting my place on the market. We do, though need some real time off to get these things properly under way. There is no rush. It will happen in time. All that matters is that we have finally found one another in the true sense and both know that for the rest of our lives we will be together; in whose house, flat or caravan it really doesn't matter.

This new sensation in my life means that although I do get twitchy with the ever-watchful eye of Maurie boring at me across the corridor, I can now take the pressure, which has lately become intense.

Normally a self-possessed person, I can actually feel my neck prickle under my high collar when that man constantly nags at me. Day in, day out. If only he could just let me get on with the job, just leave me alone, just let me breathe. His badgering is interfering with my habitual calm manner of dealing with things. I am becoming paranoid, because Maurie is putting it all on me. He has threatened to take me off the case if I don't make some progress soon. Well, no wonder I'm paranoid. I mean, who wouldn't be? His threats and harassment are simply making me sleep badly, which is not helping.

I have decided that out of order though it may be, if the super continues with what I have no doubt amounts to bullying, I will have a word with him and if that doesn't work, I will have to consider applying for a transfer.

I am unafraid of the man but he is getting under my skin

and it's starting to impede my work. I have to keep reminding myself that he is getting on and that his impending retirement might well have a bearing on his behaviour. I am quite aware that he himself is under the same kind of pressure from above. He so wants to go out in a blaze of glory as the man who led the team that caught The Keeper.

It is times like this that I really miss Mum. When she was alive, after a bad day I'd go home, plonk myself down at the kitchen table and while she was fixing supper she would know instinctively, turn to face me, cock her head on one side and say 'Well?' and I'd spill my day's worries out. She almost always had something helpful to say and would make me feel better and ready to cope the next day.

But now... Cilla is there and will listen as she always does but it doesn't feel right to burden her with these things. After all, she works a long, tiring day too. No one, not even Cilla, can ever understand how vital it is for me to get an arrest and a guilty verdict for these murders. I just have to. Especially after the cock-up with Rossi. I still can't get the super to agree to make an apology to him.

SATURDAY OCTOBER 12TH, 1996

CHAPTER FORTY-THREE

DAVID STEIN

David Stein's mood is one close to despair. Predicated on how well or badly he has done at his gambling activities that day, his moods will swing. He is only twenty-four years old, but already a hardened addict.

At the Mayfair Casino in central London tonight, he has gone with a bunch of mates and had a skinful to drink during the evening. The others all packed it in by about 1.30am, but David was doing exceptionally well on the blackjack table. Having started out with £200-worth of chips, he was £478 up so obviously had to go on playing.

One of his best friends whispered in his ear, 'Just stop now, Stein. You've done incredibly well. It's the time to stop. You know that better than anyone. You're ahead. Quit now or you'll drop the lot. You've done it before. Carry on and you'll be skint before you know it. You know you tend to do that. Please quit, Dave, and come with us.'

But David was adamant. His system was phenomenal. It was the best. He would have been crazy to stop then. They didn't know what they were talking about. He knew what he was doing.

Reluctantly, his friends gave up trying to save him from himself and left without him. He stayed and carried on winning for a couple more deals ... and then his luck began to turn. Every other bet or so he began to lose until soon it was every single card seemed to be in the dealer's favour and his profits slowly dropped deal by deal, down and down.

By the time he had only £110 left he decided to change tables and have a go at the roulette instead. So, he moved across the casino to the biggest table and put £30 on his favourite six numbers – nineteen to twenty-four. He knew this was the right thing to have done and placing £10 on odd numbers and £10 on black was, he was certain, a good move.

Whenever the croupier called '*Mesdames et messieurs, rien ne va plus,*' David's heart raced as fast as the little white ball as it spun and skittered round the roulette wheel. His eyes watched with the intensity of a cat watching its prey before it springs as the wheel slowed and the ball bobbed and bounced about until it finally shuddered to a trembling stop in the little pocket marked red, twelve.

Placing the same bets again and this time the ball landed in black twenty-eight so David lost £40 instead of £50 as the previous time. This was when he started to sweat. The fluid dripped down his face and from his armpits. His collar felt tight. He tugged at his tie to loosen it and undo the top button. He'd been up £495 at one point and look where he was at now.

He decided on one last bet. If it came good, he promised himself he'd stop and take a taxi home but if it lost, he'd have no option but to catch the Tube. Keeping £2 for the Tube back to his home in Battersea, he put the rest on the same numbers again but added £10 on the box of six numbers and £3 on odd and on black. To his despair, all the bets lost again.

By the time David lurches, furious, out of the casino, it is 3.25am, the alcohol in his system not helping his state of mind.

Fortunately, it is a mild night but David doesn't see it that way. He doesn't take in the few sounds to be heard in the city that include the small number of taxis and people still on the darkened streets. He doesn't notice anything except perhaps the pavements beneath his loafers.

He considers how unfair life can be and concerns himself with how unlucky he has been tonight. *How is it possible?* David asks himself. *I'd been doing so fucking well. Why is life so fucking unfair?*

Slightly swerving as he goes, he stumbles his way across Mayfair to Green Park Tube station where he takes a Tube on the Victoria line and gets off one stop later at Victoria, the same Tube station that poor Rob Leatham had taken a train on that fatal night earlier that year. A few late-night people are on the Tube with him but he keeps his head down, avoiding eye contact with anyone.

Once he's left the underground, passing some of the most expensive and sought-after streets in London's Belgravia on his right, young Mr Stein walks along Buckingham Palace Road, the night air helping to sober him up.

He goes along Ebury Bridge Road crossing the river over Chelsea Bridge to leave Battersea Park on his right and walk around the Queen's Circus roundabout to take Queenstown Road up towards Battersea.

The air may be sobering him up but it is making him feel even worse about losing that money tonight.

His only company, a solitary male cyclist overtakes him as he turns into Lurline Gardens. Not that the young gambler cares for any companion at this time. He just wants to be alone, go to sleep and forget his worries. He glances at his watch which reads 3.49am as he starts to walk past the large, five-storey, red-brick-and-concrete architecturally-striking period mansion blocks that dominate the street. Not far to Macduff Road where he shares a flat with a friend. Nearly home, he is feeling no less miserable or self-pitying after the walk.

The sudden unearthly sound of two cats yowling at one another in the quiet of the Battersea night echo through the streets at the same time as a grey-haired older woman in a long navy coat appears from round a corner in front of him and walks slowly toward him. She is stooping as she goes and carrying a zip bag and stops in front of him. He wonders whatever she is doing out at this hour.

Very polite, she says in a frail voice, 'I'm so sorry to trouble you but I seem to find myself lost. I'm looking for my brother's place. Could you please tell me where um...' She hesitates as she puts the bag down and carefully takes a piece of paper from her pocket that has a rough drawing of a map on it with the name of a street pencilled on it. As she is just about to show him, she drops it and when it flutters to the ground, David notices she is wearing plastic gloves. He thinks how odd that is but still bends to pick the map up. As he does so he feels her move behind him and try to put something over his head.

But she hasn't reckoned with a brown belt in Krav Maga. Even David is surprised by the speed of his own reaction. Quick as a spring, he pushes his head backward into the woman while leaning his full body-weight against her, reaching over his neck with his left arm and grabbing one of hers.

At the same time, so fast and with such deftness, he has rotated his body, punched her hard in the lower stomach with his free arm. He has kicked at her upper stomach and grabbed her other arm with both his hands while simultaneously his right leg is reaching backward to tuck itself behind and around one of her legs and trip her off her feet. In seconds he has pulled her face down onto the pavement, her left cheek scraping on concrete.

She yelps in pain while, now on top of her, David has her in his power and is blessing the day he saw *The Karate Kid*.

When he was twelve years old, he wanted to be that boy in the film. Brought up in the city of Netanya in Israel, he heard about Krav Maga, used by the Israeli Defence Forces, similar to karate but the most dangerous and non-spiritual form of quick-reaction defence from any attack where counter-attack is simultaneously employed. David started classes aged thirteen years old. Tonight those classes, which he still takes today, have saved his life.

The struggling woman lies face down under his weight, her glasses have fallen off and the knotted rope garrotte has dropped out of her right hand. Unconcerned by the drama unfolding on the street, the cats in the front are still yowling at one another and at that moment an interior light switches on and the front sash window of a ground-floor flat of one of the mansion blocks is opened.

A man leans out and shouts, 'Go away, you horrible animals, go on, piss off!' That is when by the light of a street light, he sees a young man sitting astride an old woman helpless under his strong body.

'This is not what it looks like!' David shouts at him. 'Please call the police! Call the police now! This woman has tried to kill me. I think this is the serial killer – the woman they call The Keeper! Can you get me something to tie her hands, quick! I can't hold her like this for ever. She's super strong. She was trying to kill me. I need help now, now! Please hurry!'

The woman is breathing heavily and squirming like crazy. If David had drunk less, he would be able to smell the fear oozing from her pores. She wriggles and writhes but his body weight prevents her from escaping.

The man at the window hesitates, wondering whether to believe what he is being told. It certainly doesn't look that way but David's frantic calls for help sink in, he takes a long look and sees the apparently grey-haired woman struggling with far too much strength for so old a lady and realising things are not as they seem, belts back into his flat to dial 999.

The alert goes through to Southwark Police who are known to head the search for the serial killer but also to the local Battersea police station and in her turn Detective Inspector Pollitt duly receives another night-time call from Southwark.

But all this takes time. And during this time, it begins to rain, at first gently and then in seconds there is a proper downpour.

While the man in the flat only takes a few minutes to return, to David he appears to take forever and while he struggles in the now slippery conditions to grab the woman's wrists in order to force them behind her back in readiness for tying together, it is the moment she manages to rock her body so that he is thrown slightly off balance. She is able to draw her legs up, kick back at him with both feet that are shod in flat leather-soled shoes to strike him hard in the groin and when he falls back in agony, she scrambles free, grabs her bag and sprints, a streak through the downpour. David lies moaning and crumpled in pain on the pavement.

When the man in the flat eventually comes running out of the building clutching an open umbrella, a tie and a thin leather belt, he is shocked to see David doubled up and no sign of the woman.

In a fast-gathering puddle beside the agonised young man lies a sodden rope garrotte and a pair of spectacles.

CHAPTER FORTY-FOUR

DI JO POLLITT

At about four-ish, I am sound asleep, cats curled in circles on my legs. I jump in shock, kicking them everywhere when the Nokia rings.

'Sorry,' I mumble to the animals and Cilla, forgetting she is on night duty. Attempting to clear the cigarette-related frog in my throat, my hand hunts for the mobile, a finger finally finding the button with the green symbol of a phone on the receiver. I lift the small black object to my ear and croak, 'DI Pollitt.'

The officer gives his name. Groping for the switch on the bedside lamp, I try to get my mind in focus.

'Good morning, ma'am. Sorry to wake you at such an hour but I am calling to say we've had a report from Battersea police. A man has overpowered a woman on the streets who was about to attack him from behind. He is holding her while waiting for police to come. There is a good possibility...'

'Say no more, officer... address? Quick!'

'Albert Palace Mansions, Lurline Gardens, ma'am.'

I look around for my cigarettes. I can feel my heart thumping. A sensation of needing to sit down overcomes me but of course, I am already doing so.

'I'm already there,' I say and snap off the phone. Out of bed and dressed quicker than you can say knife, there's no time for food now. He has told me back-up of eight officers in four extra cars are already on their way there and three more sent to watch the three nearest bridges over the Thames.

It's belting down with rain which doesn't help and I get sodden just getting to the Golf. I know I'm driving dangerously fast but how could I not in the circumstances? I call Tony and yell to get there soon as. Then I call Patrick. I know I shouldn't but he'd really like to know. No answer. Where is he when I need him? Dammit! I light a cig while I can. Inhale deeply.

Will this be The Keeper? Can this actually be her? I can't wait to see her but at the same time I feel prickly, slightly trembly and butterflies flutter in my stomach. The same kind of feeling as when I climbed into bed with Cilla the first time, but not. In fact, the absolute opposite. That was nervous delight and excited anticipation. To say this is nervous anticipation is grand understatement. This is petrified anticipation, except that I haven't yet turned to stone.

I get to Battersea in rapid time and the car shrieks into Lurline Gardens where I can see a couple of police cars parked up ahead and a group of people including uniformed officers gathered around the front doorsteps of a few large, turn-of-the-century mansion blocks of red brick and concrete render buildings.

My heart is hammering but before I reach them, the officers have split into pairs, run back to their cars and driven off fast down the street in opposite directions, each heading off down different side streets. Then my heart sinks and I feel sick. She has escaped.

I reach the remaining two men, skid to a halt, jump out and run to them. One is sitting on the edge of the pavement lying on his side with his knees bent up in evident pain. The other man crouches beside him looking concerned.

She can't have got far. The rain is still coming down and the men will catch her easily. She's on foot, after all. It is now obvious the grey hair was a wig worn as a disguise.

I use my mobile to call the station for more back-up as well as for an ambulance for David, who is looking green, and realise I am yelling. I speak to the DI from Battersea explaining I am in charge of the hunt for the serial killer and he graciously allows me to take charge.

I tell the officers to check the nearest Tube stations; and I tell them what she was wearing, as described by the two men; and that she may well now be blonde or, a bit of guesswork here, possibly wearing a cycling helmet. She took her bag with her which may have had a change of clothing so she may also be wearing different clothes.

The spectacles have already been bagged up by one of the constables wearing some latex gloves. David, who can manage to speak through the downpour tells me she was also wearing latex gloves – surprise, surprise.

He explains how old she appeared but of course, it was dark and she shielded her face from him as much as possible. His main impression was from her approach when she seemed to have the gait of an elderly person. She was wearing trousers and flat shoes. When he was on top of her, she was face down and it was pouring with rain, making it extra hard to see. The nearest street light was some metres away. She chose her spot well.

We know she makes use of wheelie bins and I tell Tony to scan the street for signs of them but he sees none. We have four patrol cars combing the streets of Battersea in search of one woman on foot and more are on the way. 'We'll get her, Tony,' I say with confidence. 'This is not a Hitchcock film... even though the lady has vanished once more.'

He tries to smile but fails. He minds about this as much as I do.

I have an idea she may hide in some front garden until people start to move about on the streets. Then perhaps she'll try to catch a bus. So she'll need to hide near a stop.

I leave an officer with David, go back to the Golf with Tony and cruise slowly up Lurline Gardens towards Battersea Park Road where buses travel.

The car radio crackles. An officer relays a message to say a grey wig has been found caught on a bush above a pavement on the side of Battersea Park Road heading west just beyond where Macduff Road joins it.

Wondering about this, it sounds as though it could be a red – or should I say grey – herring. I get back to the officer who found the wig and ask him exactly where it was when it was spotted. Apparently, it was just hanging on the top branch of a large garden shrub that overhung the pavement, looking as though it had been thrown high with the intention of clearing the shrub to land beyond in a front garden but had failed to do so. It was too high for anyone to easily recover.

So, after all, it looks like another slip-up from our woman. This means that she has gone west along Battersea.

We concentrate most of the cars to go that way, but knowing how cunning The Keeper is, keep a couple of cars and myself back nearer the scene of crime as she might still be lurking in this area.

Earlier, I already sent three cars to monitor Battersea, Albert and Chelsea Bridges and there is no chance she can have crossed the river on foot before our patrol cars reached the scene. The station ensured cars were sent straight to all three bridges to check, the moment they received the first call.

So, where is this effing woman? The brain cogs click forward another tooth and then it occurs. Because she was seen running on foot, we are assuming that feet are what she is on. But maybe she had a car waiting around the corner? I radio all the patrol cars and ask the question. No cars have been seen.

How about a cycle? No, no cycles. Seems we are up a very rainy creek with not a paddle in sight. But I hadn't properly interviewed David, who by now will be in the Chelsea and Westminster Hospital. I am torn between not wanting to leave this area in case something happens; and the need to speak to David. I ask Tony to stay and keep his big eyes skinned. He nods and hops out of the Golf, in which I wheel around and head for the hospital. I'll need to be quick. Siren on the roof, I race over Battersea Bridge making the A&E in double-quick time. It's still early and there is little traffic about.

Clutching my police badge, I run into A&E showing it to reception, saying it's extremely urgent that I speak with patient David Stein and a worried nurse quickly consults a list and leads the tall, soaking wet, plain-clothes policewoman to a curtained cubicle where David is still waiting to see a doctor. He looks a lot less green than he did and has at least been given a painkiller.

Getting straight to the point, I explain there is no time to waste and tell him I need to know everything he remembers before and after he was attacked.

Which bridge did he approach Lurline Gardens from when he was walking there and did he notice a car pass him on the same route? Albert Bridge, he says and no, he says, he didn't. How about a bicycle? Yes, he says, he did, but it was a man who appeared at the Queen's Circus roundabout and who went ahead of him down Lurline Gardens but he didn't notice where he turned off later.

Did he have a bag with him?

Didn't notice, says David.

Was he wearing a cycling helmet?

Yes, he was.

What colour, could he recall?

Black, he thinks or dark anyway.

And the bike? Any idea what type or colour?

Er, he did happen to notice that it was a white cycle.

And after the attack, when she was running away, she headed west, didn't she?

He thought so as that's the direction she was facing and that's the way she ran.

And did she turn off Lurline Gardens left into Macduff Road?

He was completely unaware at that point, doubled up in acute pain. If only the man who called us had been there. And where is Pickles when we need her?

I've heard enough.

Thanking him profusely, I ask if he would like me to call anyone and he gives me a friend's number which I add onto my phone and promise to ring. I wish him good luck and say I'll be in touch later, explaining I have to rush now.

Back in the Golf, I radio the patrol cars and tell them to keep their eyes skinned for a possibly male/possibly female cyclist with a black or dark helmet on a white female bike and to arrest on sight on suspicion of attempted murder.

But by the time I am back at the scene, the murderer is still unfound. Time is stealing by and it is already 5.43am.

I pick up Tony who is dripping wet, and pull in for a moment to re-engage the brain. He knows me well enough and says nothing while I smoke, sit quietly and try to think. I find myself missing Delaney. By six o'clock, I might try him again. I need his thinking. He may just have been out late. I know he'll forgive me calling so early. He has such a great way of considering life sideways.

I need the lav. Why didn't I go at the hospital when I had

the chance? Where can I go? I call the station. Ask the duty sergeant what time Battersea Park opens. Park gates at 6.30, he says. There'll be loos in there for sure. I'll just have to hang on. It's not as if I haven't had to many times before in this job. You need a trained mind, body and bladder to work in the police.

I am also missing Cilla and want to speak to her just for comfort but she'll be at the surgery and I can't call her there – or can I? I decide to take a risk but I must let her be until later... or shall I? Just a quick call now. I need the comfort of her voice.

Her mobile rings nine times. No answer, so I try the surgery number and the message machine clicks on. I explain why I called and what I'm doing and when I say goodbye and blow a kiss, I can hear my own breathlessness. I suppose my girlfriend is in with some suffering animal and can't respond.

Then I call Delaney. No reply from him either. Where the effing hell can he be? Then I remember he's not even working on this case and hasn't been for a while. He could be anywhere.

God, my bladder is about to burst. My watch tells me it's after 6am. The rain is slowing to a drizzle. Tony and I get out of the Golf and walk either side of the road slowly down Lurline Gardens back towards Queen's Circus. One of the patrol cars is cruising the other way past us and another is stationary at the end of where Queenstown Road joins the Circus roundabout. If it was The Keeper wearing a helmet on the bike David saw (easy to mistake for a bloke if not wearing the coat) then she had come from this direction and surely would want to go back this way.

We keep our eyes peeled. He on the right, I the left. On my side I pass a number of similar mansion blocks to the one David was attacked outside, most of which have large shrubs or hedges adorning front gardens behind low brick walls. While Tony walks and scans on the other side, passing big Victorian houses, I carefully study each as I pass for signs of plastic gloves or anything else that she might have thrown away. And then, suddenly there it is! Behind a high evergreen bush a well-hidden cream-coloured woman's cycle leans up against it, a helmet hanging on the handlebars. There is no way the cars would ever have seen it. Such luck I walked past and looked behind.

Under our noses all the time. And the wig *was* a red herring after all. She must have removed the coat, worn the helmet into which she would have tucked the blonde hair, doubled back and nipped down side streets watching like the vixen that she is for her chance to get back to Lurline Gardens.

So where has the lady fox gone now? The cycle is close to the entrance of this particular building. She has probably had the gall to ring a bell and gain entry on false pretences. In which case, she has either slipped out of the back, or she is somewhere in the building. I radio all the cars to come at once, some to go round the back and the fingerprint boys as well – the quicker the prints on the bike are run through the system the better chance we have of finding who she is.

One thing I know, she's not far – that's for sure. She's not getting her bike back either, that's for sure as well.

I let out a deep sigh and suddenly feel exhausted as well as needing the lav, I have to sit down. My bladder aches and much as I need a pee, I am starting to crave a coffee. I notice that the rain has kindly stopped and sit down on the low, wet brick wall outside the block waiting until all the cars have appeared.

When they do, I tell the boys, and one woman, to be ready for a major search of the building.

At the front entrance of the five-storey building, happy that Tony is by my side again, I ring one of the ground-floor-flat doorbells. I glance at my watch again, mindful that I must call David's friend. I decide to give this job to Tony and pass the number to him while waiting for a response to the entry-phone. I buzz it again, twice.

Finally, a furious female voice answers, 'What the hell is

this? That's the second time tonight! What the hell are you doing waking me up again?'

'This is Detective Inspector Pollitt of the Southwark Police here, madam. I am extremely sorry to have to wake you so early but this is a matter of considerable importance and I would be grateful if you would allow me entry. Thank you, madam.'

I stand back and wait. Within a few seconds, a curtain twitches at the corner of a front bay window and an angry, sandy-haired middle-aged woman peers through. I show her my badge at the window and our group that consists of Tony and me and six uniformed officers.

Within a minute, the overweight, bleary-eyed woman wearing a pink dressing gown has let us in and after a few questions from a keyed-up DI, has explained that about a quarter of an hour or so earlier she was woken by some over-made-up blonde woman claiming to have forgotten her keys. She saw her through the window as she wasn't going to let any old bod into the building, but the woman seemed genuine.

'Just because I happen to live in the front flat, it's so unfair that everyone wakes me up,' grouses Miss Bull as I discover she is aptly named. It's going to take a lot to make her happy but frankly, at this point in time I couldn't care less.

Having sent the rest of the men to comb the building all my mind is focused on is to have a pee before my bladder detonates. I simply raise myself to my full height and ask our disgruntled hostess if she might allow me to use her toilet. Once that's accomplished, I am ready for action again.

I now explain the full circumstances to Miss Bull. While she listens, she pulls her dressing gown tie a little tighter and fusses with her uncombed curls, her eyes widening, her manner rapidly altering to alert helpfulness as she grasps that she is not only a witness in the search for the infamous Keeper but that she actually saw her and spoke to her on the entry-phone.

I can see her imagining accepting offers of large sums from Sunday papers for interviews and being hassled by TV crews for her take on the case.

After a twenty-minute search of the block in which I take part, no sign is found of the woman so I decide she must have slipped out of the back of the building, perhaps to wait for the Battersea Park gates to open at 6.30am where she might be able to hide and get away from us.

It is just at this moment that I receive a call from the custody sergeant on duty at Southwark telling me two constables have brought in a prisoner and does he want me to do the formal arrest and charge or should he do it himself and it is The Keeper. He deliberately kept the mention of The Keeper until the end.

My heart bumps into overdrive and I don't know whether to be ecstatic, angry or confused. A mix of all three, I am hardly able to respond. My strict instructions were that if she were caught, to arrest, cuff, hold her and immediately inform me so I had the chance to see her before sending her to Southwark.

But then, come on Jo, I tell myself, so the constables made a mistake – Battersea boys presumably – but we've got her! We've actually caught The Keeper. This is something. In fact, this is something incredible. This is something just amazing. I tell the sergeant to keep the prisoner under heavy security and armed guard in a closed cell. I specifically ask him to leave her in the clothes she was caught in. I want the super and others to see what we have caught. And, I add, he's right, I want the honour of charging her myself.

'Not a word,' I warn, 'not a word is to get out to the press. Southwark is in charge of this case and Detective Chief Superintendent Green will see to it that anyone will be in serious trouble if there are any leaks whatsoever. I am on my way now.'

The sergeant starts to say something, but I cut him short, telling him I have to get on and whatever he has to say, he can tell me later.

I return to the Golf and without warning, suddenly feel incredibly tired. I sit in the car with Tony beside me and remain still for a few moments while I smoke and allow the giddy feeling to wash over me.

I am a detective inspector whose long hunt for a major serial killer is over. Hardly able to believe it is true, as the news sinks in and my heart slows, the sensation of exhaustion gradually lifts to one of elation as I begin to feel proud of the hard work the enormous team have done in their endeavours to capture such an elusive character. Feeling a great deal better than earlier, I switch on the engine and head to the station. We all need something to eat, let alone some shut-eye. The food is essential but the shut-eye will have to wait.

My training has taught me how to calm myself in readiness to face this killer but it is still a scary thought. No police like the idea of interviewing weirdos, let alone serial killers. This is my first and I am nervous, there is no getting away from it. I fish about for the rescue remedy in my bag and quite a few droplets hit my tongue.

When I get to a red light, I check myself in the rear mirror, I tell myself I'll manage just as I always do. Mum smiles and nods at me in my head.

When I arrive at the station at 6.49am, the custody sergeant is all smiles. 'Morning, ma'am.' He seems anxious.

'What a very bright, sunny day it is today, sarge, even if the sun isn't up yet. As you know we have a highly important guest here in Southwark. I very much look forward to putting a face and a name to the lady.'

'I think you may be...'

I interrupt him, 'Sorry, sergeant, I have to nip to my office. Back in five. Come on, Tony.'

The hunt for this killer has been a long... what was it? Fifteen months and in that time, I have come to rely on the detective sergeant. His presence by my side has bolstered my bravado throughout the hunt and what he lacks in education is more than made up for by his innate intelligence and outstanding common sense.

He is kind-hearted too and I feel he has looked out for his boss, from which I have drawn strength when times have been as tough as they have been during the past year.

We go to my office where I have a mini-fridge in which I always keep a piece of cheddar cheese, some sausage rolls and milk. I also have a supply of biscuits and crisps and apples for emergencies such as this. And I have a kettle, some teabags, some instant coffee, sugar and some milk. Before we clap eyes on the perpetrator of five hideous crimes that have involved our lives for over a year, we need sustenance. We are tired and have empty bellies that need some fuel in them. Big Tony needs his filling even more than I do.

The man positively wolfs down a large chunk of cheddar, a couple of bags of crisps, a number of biscuits and two apples in record quick time as he also gulps down a mug of steaming coffee.

Much as I crave one now, I tell myself to lay off the coffee until later, I'm already jittery enough. I have a hot cup of tea, a chunk of cheddar, a bag of crisps, three biscuits, one last cig and I take an apple with me in my bag.

I practise some deep breathing with Tony as we steel ourselves for our look at the murderess in the cell. I'll interview her later once I've spoken to Maurie.

We go back down to the cells and wait for the sergeant to let us through the locked door to the cell where our woman is incarcerated. I peer through the peephole and it takes a while to find the prisoner, who is sitting on the end of the bed.

I hear a cry of shock that has actually come from me as I have lost my balance and Tony has caught me before I fall. I clutch his arm for support.

My heart races and I feel sick and giddy. The figure on the bed has heard and when I have recovered enough to look again, they are staring at the peephole. The long, dark-blue woman's coat is open over a white shirt, a pair of trousers and flat black lace-ups. A blonde wig lies on the bench beside the figure, their own dark hair plastered to the head under a hairnet.

My mouth falls open. I feel myself go pale. I look away and back again to peer at the weird sight in front of me.

'Hello Jo. Is that you?'

I am literally dumbstruck as I stare at the face.

Eyes surrounded by heavy black eyeliner glitter as they settle on me. Lips caked with pink crack apart to reveal yellow teeth. The thick stagey make-up exaggerates an unnerving look about the facial features.

I have to go and sit down; I am so stunned. Trying to collect my thoughts, I mumble, 'Er, um, I'll see you later.'

'Oh Jo, I was so hoping to talk to you now. I really need to explain a few things.'

I can't be seen. That's something. 'Oh, I'm not sure you can very readily explain away murdering five and almost six young men. We'll talk later.'

'The P was for Pollitt and the kisses were for you, Jo.'

I feel sick. I sink onto a chair in the corridor.

'Your turn, Tony.'

When he looks through the peephole, like me, Tony does a double take. The second time, he stamps the floor with his feet and shouts, 'Blouse and skirt! Puppa Jeezus! Blow Puppa Jeezus! I don' believe my eyes, man. It can' be!'

'It is, Tony, it is.'

'Bu'... bu'... Puppa Jeezus! Something wrong here. It can' be.'

'I know. It's incredible, isn't it?'

All Tony can do is shake his big head. He takes another look. 'Well, man, tha's the mos...'

Nausea rising in my throat, I run down the corridor and only just make it to the ladies in time before throwing up.

I go back to my office to try to collect my thoughts. I must look bemused because I am. I cannot think straight. In fact, I can barely speak. Mum comes to the rescue yet again. *Come on, Jo,* she says. *One deep breath and you can do this standing on your head.* She looks me full in the face and smiles that wonderful smile of hers. When Tony knocks, I rise to my feet. His uncomplicated approach to the situation is just what I need to see and hear and with Mum and him beside me, shocked though I am, I am not alone and I now feel ready to face the foe. I want to hug Tony but instead, give him a high-five.

'Come on, let's go take a look at what's in that bag.'

I bustle past him and head for the incident room to seek out the exhibits officer.

'I believe you have a bag brought in with this morning's homicide arrest.'

The officer says, 'I do, ma'am.'

'I need to look inside it before we interview the prisoner. Do you need to come with me when I look at it?'

'It's essential that none of the evidence is contaminated, ma'am. We don't want to give the defence any cause for complaint.'

'We definitely do not. Is it okay to open it, please?'

The woman says, 'I have to be with you when you do so, ma'am. It's procedure. I'm sorry.'

'I know. Don't worry.'

'I'll get it right away.'

'Bring it to the interview room. We'll do it in there.'

A pernickety woman, her job demanding it, she hands Tony and I a pair of latex gloves each, also putting some on before she disappears to collect the bag from where it is stored. She soon returns to the empty interview room carrying the black zip holdall and places it on the table.

Unsure of what I might find, I gingerly unzip the bag and remove the contents one by one, laying them carefully on the table.

The first thing is a box of identical latex gloves to the ones we are wearing. Next, a lady's two-sided hand mirror with a magnifying side and an ordinary one. There is a large make-up bag containing a skin cream, a small plastic carton of blue eye shadow, an eyebrow stick, a black eyeliner, a black mascara, a stick of thick matt stage foundation that actors wear, some pink lipstick, a powder compact, eye make-up remover, a make-up remover and cotton wool balls. In addition there is a super sharp surgeon's knife in a sheath.

There is a screw-top jar containing some liquid that I guess is maybe formaldehyde in readiness to preserve the genitals – I'm not opening that for certain just in case – nasty stuff, formaldehyde. A pair of rubber gloves and some goggles verify my feeling as correct. No need for a covering as the plastic mac would have done the job there.

Lastly, there is a packet of empty zipped plastic bags to keep the jar safe inside. Nothing if not efficient, this filthy rotten killer.

I am grateful to my brain for already making the leap to thinking of the inmate as this. For a moment I feel stupid. Duped, fooled, taken for an idiot and I want to burst into tears. But then I realise we are all in the same boat. Everyone who worked closely with this killer will feel like me.

Don't take it to heart, I tell myself as I gaze at the objects on the table. The murderer's a psycho. It hurts so much and I feel so hurt that someone I trusted without question could have turned out to be a bloody murderer. I have to wrestle with my mind to convince myself that there was nothing personal about it.

Replacing the items carefully in the holdall, I hand it back to the exhibits officer. 'We'll be needing this again shortly. Please keep it safe, officer. Thank you.'

'Of course, ma'am.'

Maurie has been buzzing me incessantly since he arrived but I've been ducking his calls. I am absolutely not prepared to have him barking at me before I have even spoken with the prisoner. Now I am going to interview them, I can drop the bombshell. I ring Green and tell him who it is.

'Bloody hell! No, Jo. Sorry, but you've got it wrong. It can't be. It simply can't be. Have you gone mad? Bloody hell! Are you sure, woman?'

'As eggs is eggs, Maurie, it is. Amazing, isn't it?'

'But how the bloody hell...?'

'I know. It's just so shocking. It's, as you would say, Maurie, bloody marvellous.'

'Bloody hell, Jo Pollitt. I just cannot believe it. I have to get down to cells and take a look for myself. This is just preposterous. It really is. Are you having me on?'

'That I am not. Go and take a look for yourself. But for heaven's sake let me get the interview done first before you do a press release, sir. They will go crazy, completely crazy. This is a scandal. There's so much to be done. We'll need the shrink down here soon as – the offender's clearly mad as a box of frogs. Funny, you know, I almost saw it and I did wonder but when a person is so good at their job and so good at trying to help us...' I stop myself as I remember, 'but then of course, all the time they weren't. Oh God! There is so much to learn. There will be textbooks written about this case. Psychological experts will obsess over this as they try to work this killer out, whose brain has to be one of the most curious ever...'

'Don't give tuppence about the bloody brain,' interrupts Maurie. 'It's the crime I care about. Killed five young men in their prime, Jo and almost a sixth. It's an appalling and tragic affair. The sooner this creature is put away for life the better. Shame they did away with the death penalty if you ask me. People like that don't deserve to live.'

God, I think, *he'll be off on one of his rants if I'm not careful.*

'Yes, well, I must get on, no doubt you'll want to watch the interview. I'm going in five minutes with DS Smith, who by the way has been brilliant all the way through and I'll be recommending him for a promotion, sir.'

'Jolly good. Good luck, Jo. I'll get down there right away then I'll go and watch your interview. Well done, Jo, just absolutely bloody marvellous!'

CHAPTER FORTY-FIVE

The first thing I ask is did he murder others before he took over as the HO pathologist.

Dr Flynn, polite as ever, says that he didn't and that the idea of releasing young men from their burden only came to him when he was given the job. He wanted to be sure to care for them afterwards and to ensure their new-found freedom was as full of love and as happy as it should be.

He openly admits to all the murders although he doesn't seem to accept that that is what they were. When I refer to them as killings or murders, he corrects me and calls them 'releases'. His mind is truly unhinged and yet he has been able to convince us all along that he was working so well on the cases.

It's just mind-boggling to think that he was doing autopsies on his own victims. So improbable is this result that it is hard for the reality to sink in. Of course, his job was the perfect alibi. I suppose it was what he wanted... to have their bodies as close to him as possible. I ask him and he says he was by far the best person to care for 'his boys' as he calls them.

Flynn seems strangely unaffected by being caught. He is unworried by anything much except when it comes to the trophies about which he suddenly becomes extremely precious. He will not reveal their whereabouts.

If they're in his house, which I am certain they will be as they are so precious to him, we shall find them. They evidently mean a huge amount to him. Delaney did always say they would. It's bizarre. Presumably they are all he has left of his boys.

Flynn's attitude appears to be a mass of contradictions. While he gives the impression of caring little that he will spend the rest of his life in prison, he all along took some trouble into fooling us that he was a female.

If psychopath he is, he seems unusually straight about revealing everything about the details and perfectly at ease to tell us all about the first murder and how he deliberately chose the night before he was due to take a morning flight abroad to Minorca for a fortnight's holiday, giving him the best possible alibi if there ever was a chance that he slipped up in any way.

Describing exactly how he dressed as a woman in a PVC mac, he readily explains this was to put me and the Met on the wrong foot and that it also prevented blood from getting onto his clothes. These macs were cheap, he explains and could be thrown away after use. He cheerfully describes how he stalked his victims, approached them, showed them the trick piece of paper, deliberately dropped it, got behind them when they bent down to pick it up, threw the garrotte over their bent heads, kneed them in the back and so forth.

The shrinks will have a field day with this one. In my view he seems to be at least two or more completely different people – but what do I know? Only that he's a very strange fellow who has pulled the wool over our eyes successfully and that if he hadn't happened upon a Krav Maga brown belt he would still be doing so. I don't know if we ever would have caught him. The words *cunning* and *manipulative* don't start to describe him. He seems to be able to switch personalities when it suits.

After probably the most gruelling day of my life when I get back to the safety and comfort of Cilla's arms that evening I am so exhausted, I can barely put one foot in front of the other. My girlfriend cooks, cossets and cares for me and I am so grateful and feel so blessed to have her in my life. After a couple of Cosmos and a delicious chicken casserole with some glasses of red wine, Cilla sits next to me on the sofa. She puts an arm round my shoulders. Tears inch down my cheeks. She holds me close and I can feel she is close to crying too.

'You cry it out, my darling,' she says. 'This is relief as much as anything. I know what you've been through. There's been so much on your shoulders. You've caught a serial killer who you believed was on your side. You have been through a plethora of emotions recently and have all the reasons in the world to have a good blub.'

She shifts her position and reaches into her handbag that is on the floor beside the sofa. Pulling out a couple of tissues, she hands one to me and blows her own nose with the other.

'Unless, of course,' she continues, 'you're crying over my chicken casserole?'

I laugh through the tears and snot, wipe my eyes and drop my head onto my woman's shoulder.

MID-OCTOBER TO MID-NOVEMBER, 1996

CHAPTER FORTY-SIX

DR PHOEBE FLYNN

P hoebe Flynn suffers from intense shock when she learns what her husband has been doing on some of those late nights when she had thought he was working. Interviewed by the police, she tells them that she tended to take the reins when it came to the organisation of their lives.

Edward, she says, is (or was) a workaholic. At his happiest in the midst of an autopsy, he believes people like him are needed, for they are content to be doing something that most people would find abhorrent. From his point of view, once you came to understand the beauty of the workings of the human form it became a fascination that would take you over.

Back to the previous July, Phoebe had insisted that they both needed a proper holiday and some of what she called 'R and R'.

She recalls Edward saying he was doing last-minute work at the mortuary, and that he only returned home at four in the morning, which gave him an hour before they drove to Heathrow to catch their flight to Minorca, where they arrived at their hotel by mid-morning.

She says he behaved completely normally, showing no signs of being flustered or het-up and that she can barely believe he had just returned from committing such a heinous murder.

She does remember him going up to the attic 'to look for his old cricket cap' which he said was in a trunk up there. He said he wanted to bring it to keep the sun off his face. When he came back down, he didn't have it with him, saying he couldn't find it.

She also recalls the next day in the morning when they were relaxing side by side on poolside loungers, Edward was deep into reading a number of British newspapers he'd collected from the hotel. On the front page of one, under the main headline, he showed her a story. She even recollects the shocking caption:

Father of three strangled and castrated in Lambeth

Normally a measured, self-composed man who rarely displayed irritation, Edward apparently admitted to being thoroughly annoyed that this extraordinary murder had taken place on his patch and that there he was – abroad.

She remembers what she now knew to be feigned, his chagrin at missing such a bizarre murder and that this was the kind of twisted, dangerous killer a forensic expert aspired to help capture.

What incredibly elaborate lengths this killer went to, in order to ensure no suspicion would ever fall on him. As if anyone would have ever thought it could be the pathologist on the case.

She was able to shed some light on how Edward had been physically strong enough to commit the murders with seemingly no trouble. The couple were both keen on keeping themselves as fit as possible. At their house in Battersea, they had installed a miniature gym in one of the four bedrooms where they both worked out when they had time. Edward lifted weights and both used the treadmill and a state-of-the-art cross-trainer.

He would say that he had too often seen close-up the results that lack of exercise can have on bodies and, aware of how much time he spent either standing over them, hunched over cadavers or microscopes or hanging about in courtrooms, how necessary it was for him to keep as fit as he could.

Phoebe, who in her job as dermatologist deals with everything from appalling cases of acne to acute sebaceous dermatitis, knows well the importance of keeping mind and body healthy.

Although a private person by nature, she has agreed to discuss their sexual relationship with a psychiatrist employed by the crown prosecution.

She tells him that they married when they were very young. Both of them were virgins and surprisingly ignorant about sex. The first year she found it strange that he only wanted to have sex perhaps once a month or so and this always felt somewhat forced, as though he was doing it out of duty rather than desire.

Phoebe had girlfriends and they talked about that sort of thing but because she was a bit embarrassed about how minimal their sex life was, after she married, she tended to avoid the subject.

The psychiatrist asks her whether she would be able to say whether Edward ejaculated.

She blushes and replies that she doesn't believe he ever did and says the act was always over very fast.

He then asks her about the second year of the marriage to which she replies, 'Yes, well naturally since we had agreed not to have children, it tailed off. I suppose it might have been about twice a year or so for the next couple of years and then it just stopped altogether. I think Edward only really ever did it for me as I honestly don't think he enjoyed it at all. Until recently, I knew so little about sex but now that I have experienced a proper love affair, I realise that he had more than just a low sex drive. I now know that he had no sex drive as far as I was concerned. I am certain that he must actually be gay.'

'Did you suspect as much before you learnt what you now know?'

'I must admit I didn't. It never occurred to me.

'In your opinion, was there an event you believe that may have pushed Edward over the edge into becoming a murderer?'

'His mother's death. One hundred per cent. He adored her and was deeply affected by it. She was an awful woman, you know.'

'In what way was she awful?'

'Perhaps I exaggerate. But I really do blame her for Edward's descent into this madness of his. She dominated him so absolutely and smothered him with such a fierce, possessive love to the point where the only thing he could do was to put her on a pedestal in order to cope with her demands of him. She was incredibly demanding of Edward.'

'What sort of demands did she make of him?'

'Her expectations of him were heaped upon his young shoulders. She pushed and pushed him. It was tantamount to bullying. And it was all for her own glorification so that she could boast about her wonderful son who was a doctor.'

In Phoebe's opinion, the mother was a self-serving woman who had Edward wrapped around her little finger.

Phoebe gives the psychiatrists as much background information as she knows about Edward's childhood. But it soon becomes clear that she only knows the Edward he was prepared to show her. That he had not shared his innermost thoughts is abundantly clear.

He was an only child who had been frightened of his father

but had never explained why; only that the man had been rough with his mother.

His father had died in a car accident when Edward was seven years old. The child had been in the front seat of the car, his father driving. A lorry in front of them had lost its load of metal pipes and one had gone through the windscreen on the driver's side. The father had swerved and hit a tree on the opposite side of the road. He had been impaled on a pipe that had run through his stomach.

The child had suffered a broken collarbone and had been badly bruised and cut up. By far the worst thing was that trapped in the car, he had had to sit next to his dying father for some time before help had arrived.

After the father's death, the boy had become inseparable from his mother who had just about run his life for him. Edward had apparently not shared his mother's sense of loss of his father.

Phoebe believes he became jealous of his late father's place in his mother's eyes and that the trauma he went through sitting in the car beside him had in some way affected his brain to commence the process that ended as it so tragically did.

Mrs Flynn Senior had died from cancer three years previously.

With regard to his marriage, he had originally ideated his wife as a romantic sweetheart rather than a sexual person.

Phoebe Flynn confirms that he very occasionally went through the physical actions of sexual intercourse with her, she now believes, purely for her sake.

She has long since understood that he was not interested in her sexually but that she was certain he was fond of her and had no particular desire to leave her nor to look elsewhere for sexual comfort. She has always felt that he had little interest in sex and a very low sex drive.

She openly admits to having had a love affair with a doctor who works at the same hospital as she and says that in the past year or so Edward has been acting so strangely and has spent so little time at home, that she doubts he would even have noticed or cared if she had told him about her romance.

CHAPTER FORTY-SEVEN

DI JO POLLITT

A month or so after the capture of Flynn, I call Delaney and ask if he'll meet me for another of those "delicious" dishes of scampi and chips in the Red Lion in Southwark. He's happy to do so and I am equally pleased to see him saunter in wearing his usual outfit of faded jeans and boots, his leather coat swinging as he walks.

When he sees me sitting on a stool at the bar, he waves cheerfully. 'Hi there, good to see you, Jo.' He hugs then pecks me on both cheeks. 'How's you doing? Must be so damn glad that one's been put to bed at last. What a nutter he turned out to be. Sorry I wasn't much help in the end.'

'Good to see you too, Delaney. You got a lot closer than most of us. At least you thought it might be a female. What are you having?'

'Some female! Half a pint of bitter, please.' He jumps up onto the barstool next to mine. We don't bother chatting about other stuff but go straight to the subject that has brought us together in the first place.

He is hungry for what I can tell him but before I get started, he says, 'We should thank Jesus, Mary and Joseph for that karate man, heh? It's the usual story with serial killers that are too clever to get caught by the police. It always seems to be a mix of arrogance and bad luck that finally brings about their downfall. In this case, another man's irritation with pussycats and his inadvertent intervention...'

'I know, without those animals, who knows how long this could have gone on?'

But he replies looking me straight in the eyes, 'Can't have been easy for you, inspector.'

He has only ever called me inspector in an ironic or teasing kind of way. And I cannot hold his gaze as I try to sound casual. 'Oh no, Delaney, I am just so bloody grateful he got caught.'

He smiles, reaches out a flat hand and gently pats my arm. 'So am I, so am I.'

We talk about how Edward had used the Northern line underground to get to places where he stalked his prey. He told us in the interviews that it took him conveniently back close to his house in Battersea.

'Tell me Jo, what have they concluded so far about him?'

'As you know, Edward has been completely helpful to us. Apart from being a dual personality, the shrinks have also recognised he is an asexual which they explain is a sexual orientation, like being gay or straight. It's neither celibacy nor abstinence.

'Apparently, asexual people can have romantic attractions and may identify themselves as straight, gay or bisexual and can form committed relationships and value all the non-sexual benefits of a partnership that sexual individuals enjoy but just without the sex.'

Delaney looks taken aback and says as much. 'A surprising result,' he murmurs and after a long pause continues, 'So, I suppose then that his reasons for castrating his victims must have been to neutralise them rather than anything other...'

I interrupt him, 'Edward insists his motive was for the *good* of the young men. To "help" them find *real* love, was his purpose. Apparently, he held some twisted belief that he loved his victims... I mean, *what*? You kill some random young man and *then* you *love* them? It's not as though he turned out to be a necrophiliac.'

Patrick examines his glass of beer while he absorbs what I am saying. He replies slowly, 'So, given the fact that he is asexual, I think we now need to try to understand that he could only love them once he had removed their sexual parts. That was when he was able to love them fully. Once they became nonsexual as it were.'

'Then why kill them in the first place?'

'To render them sexless, he had to. I mean who's going to agree to allow him to castrate them for his mad beliefs? He genuinely ached for love. But romantic love only. Love that did not and could not include any prospect of sexual involvement. Phoebe had disappointed since she was a sexual being.

'He ended up doing what all serial killers do, which was to act out his fantasies. The so-called trophies turned out not to be trophies at all. They were kept only as the last bodily part of the people he had killed after they were buried or cremated. The parts were not kept as a reminder of the men's sexuality but as a reminder of their,' he held up two crooked fingers on both hands to indicate inverted commas, '"lives" together with him.'

'And why, since he was married to a female, did he choose to kill boys?'

'Easier to render them androgynous. You can't simply chop something off a woman to neutralise her. She has a womb and ovaries – complicated stuff to remove on the streets and disfiguring to boot.'

I pull a face.

'Besides, young men represent sexuality at its most potent and in Edward's eyes, that is the most threatening. With a male you can simply and quickly get rid of the meat and two veg and Bob's your sexless uncle...'

'Patrick, you really do have a way with words.'

'Well thank you, inspector.' He grins that naughty blue-eyed grin of his.

We order some scampi in a basket and carry on analysing the bizarre case we shared for a time. However many times we try to come up with why Edward Flynn turned from pathologist to murderer or rather managed to be both pathologist and murderer of his own victims we could only explain it as thrill-taking.

That he must have got tremendous thrills not only from fooling us all but also from having his own victims in his mortuary for him to 'work on'.

We talk about how extraordinary Flynn's ability was to remain so alert and energetic when on the days when he was performing autopsies; he had been up most of the previous night committing murder, so could only have managed an hour or so sleep at the most before being called to the scenes of his own crimes.

A truly astonishing human, Dr Edward Flynn. Before we part company, Delaney and I promise to meet at least twice a year as friends if nothing else.

Before I go, Delaney mentions Rossi. 'I can't help feeling bad about poor Marco, you know. We did put him through the wringer, didn't we?'

'We did,' I agree, 'and what is more, we had a letter of complaint from a solicitor we think Rossi got through the Citizens Advice Bureau demanding reparations for the damage to his flat. And you know what?' Delaney cocks his head. 'Get this: Maurie himself actually visited the man with a formal letter of apology plus a cheque to make good his flat following our search.'

'Jesus, Mary and Joseph!' says Delaney.

EPILOGUE

In the course of finding evidence before Edward Flynn was brought to trial at the Old Bailey, the police made a thorough search of his house in Battersea.

In the attic under three floorboards, they found an ancient, slim, illustrated booklet entitled *The Merciful Garrotte* and laid on its side a gallon container of formaldehyde.

In a plastic container next to it, they retrieved a pair of laboratory tongs, a box of latex gloves, a pack of seven black plastic long lady's raincoats, some packets of pull-on, knee-high, black stocking-socks and a box of cheap, plastic, black, low-heeled ladies' court shoes size eight.

A pair of goggles, an apron and some rubber gloves lay on top of a separate plastic lidded box, which when opened revealed five pickling jars in a neat row carefully labelled in immaculate writing with the first names of the victims. Winston, Ahmad, Jim, Rob, Jack. Beside them an unmarked sixth headed an ominous new row awaiting more to join alongside it. A cardboard box of what had been twenty-four screw-top jars with six removed was tucked alongside the gallon container.

It took hundreds of thousands of man hours of work before the killer known as The Keeper was finally caught. A great deal of pressure, stress and anguish was put on all of the many men and women involved in the capture.

DI Jo Pollitt

The relief I feel from seeing Flynn behind bars cannot be underestimated. After long months of chequered sleep, anxiety and self-doubt, I can at last relax and get back to the usual business of my job. Not to say that there aren't more murders and crimes to keep me on my toes, because there most certainly are. But nothing will ever take its toll on me in the way those serial killings did.

Now, as well, I have some time. I want to search for Cilla's rapist and I gently ask her whether she would like me to see if I can find any new leads that might help trace the man. She is all for it. It is brave of her to face such a traumatic memory again, and I say as much. She doesn't think it brave at all; she thinks it is the right thing to do since the possibility remains that he may still be out there committing violent attacks on other young girls. If he is, he needs catching, locking up and the key throwing away.

It will be a very long shot since it happened twenty-five years ago but the crime will have been bagged up in the records of the evidence room. It happened before the arrival of the DNA database so if there is any physical evidence, which Cilla thinks there might be, then there's a slim chance we could get somewhere. I don't push her on what she thinks the police may have kept as she is naturally hazy. She has blocked much of the trauma from her memory.

But Cilla is determined that I should try to see if any progress ever was made on the case. There certainly wasn't any she ever heard of. Over the past months since telling me about it, having unburdened herself of the weight of such a secret for so long, she is calm and rational when talking about it and I am so pleased for her that at last she has been able to open up. I can tell how much better she feels as a result.

'If the perpetrator is still on the outside, he poses a significant risk to women and in particular, to teenage girls. It would be so good to know whether he has been caught or if not whether he still could be and locked up for a lengthy period of time.' She sounds like a textbook. Perhaps some time back she read a booklet about rape. The words almost sound rehearsed. But I understand why. This method of talking about it creates a distance for her.

The crime occurred within the Hackney police area. The station had moved their evidence records that are over ten years old to a warehouse in the East End. So that is where I go.

A spooky, echoey place, a huge musty chamber full of metal shelving stacked high with row upon row of cardboard boxes marked with case numbers, I search through the evidence room looking for Cilla's case. I'm on a wing and a prayer that in her file there just might be something that nowadays could lead us to an arrest. The likelihood is slim as we don't even have a name for the rapist – but DNA is what I have in mind, of course. A lot of advances have been made since 1971.

I find the box marked Cilla Pelham in which there is her torn school shirt, torn panties and school skirt. My heart turns over to see these wretched items, like ones I once wore too. They have stayed in polythene bags in this box for so long, testaments to a grossly violent act that gave some voracious bastard a short-lived thrill but almost ruined a young girl's life for ever. For if my Cilla were not the strong, courageous character that she is, she might well have buckled under and not have lived a normal life from that day on.

'You know,' she said to me when we sat down and thrashed the whole thing out, 'the worst thing about it was neither the physical pain nor the fear, although both were bad; the *worst* thing was going to the police. It was so humiliating being examined and them taking my clothes and all the questions they asked. It was just so awful.'

I felt relieved that we, meaning the police, are better at understanding how to handle cases of rape nowadays, although there is still much room for improvement. But I dread to think what it must have been like in those times. Awful I should imagine and handled with just about zero sensitivity.

I read through the file which is carefully written in fountain pen. Lower down the page it indicates that semen was found on the skirt. When I read this, my hearts leaps.

There is a laughable identikit picture the police had put together following Cilla's description of the man. It looks like a child's bad drawing. The detective in me longs to show this to the grown-up Cilla and ask if she can recall the man's face and if so, how accurate the picture is, but the woman who loves her does not want to put her through such a thing.

I decide to mention it and let her lead the way on that one.

A clear chain of custody must follow the evidence at all times and when I take the clothing and files out of the evidence room, this all must be logged and I am responsible for keeping them secure.

As soon as, I send the clothing off for tests and ask for it all to be tested for possible signs of hair or anything else that may be relevant.

The tests come back and bingo! We have the rapist's DNA. Blood pressure pumping, I rush it over to the National DNA Database on the slim chance of finding a match. Only samples from convicted criminals, or people awaiting trial are on it and it was only started last year so we'll be lucky if we find one. When a new profile is submitted, the records are automatically searched for matches between individuals and unsolved crime-stain records. These records are also searched for matches to others so it links both individuals to crimes and crimes to crimes.

Meantime, I have plenty of other cases to keep me busy. The crack cocaine epidemic is raging and the Met is at full stretch trying to deal with it.

When the DNA results come back, there is no match. So that avenue is a dead end. I am so disappointed as that was the best hope. The next thing I can do is hunt through other cases of similar rapes of teenagers around the same time that Cilla's occurred. Presumably, the Hackney coppers did that then with no luck, and would have continued to watch out for them for some time.

My problem is I really don't have enough time to give. To completely reopen this cold case, I would need substantial reason to give the super. The fact that Cilla is my new live-in lover is probably not substantial enough and knowing Maurie and his prejudices, it wouldn't exactly go down a storm.

She and I will have to live with it and tell ourselves that at least we have each other and that she's come through it remarkably well. As they say, you can't win 'em all.

It's a real shame, though when I retire in however many years' time, I'll hunt the effing bastard down then. I make myself that promise, so that's two bastards on my 'to deal with' list. But Mum's killer, when he's eventually out, will take top priority.

Dr Edward Flynn

I played it extremely well, as usual. I outwitted all of them all along and if it hadn't been for those damned cats, I'd never have been caught. They think they understand me. They think they've got my psyche worked out. They may know Edward, but they haven't reckoned with me.

Because my father died and Mamma brought me up, they

think that affected Edward in some way. They have no idea. They think I was changed by sitting in the car next to my dead father. But they don't know what I saw my father do to my poor mother. They think I have told them everything but they would be wrong there. Edward has told them what they need to hear – but I haven't.

I suppose I was only four, five and six at the time. I saw them once and that was proof that my monster of a father regularly raped my poor darling Mummy. I went to their bedroom one night because I'd had a nightmare and was scared and I went into their room and he was on top of her and she was moaning and squealing and calling out and he had a hand over her mouth and was telling her 'shh' while he was forcing himself and pushing away on top of her so rough and cruel.

When they saw me, of course he stopped at once and rolled off Mummy. But it was too late, I had seen his crime.

After that, many nights when I couldn't sleep, I would creep to their bedroom and would hear them from behind their closed door. So many times I almost ran in to try and stop him but I was frightened to. They don't know I witnessed it many times. I wanted to try to help Mummy but I was scared to go into the room.

I never forgave that horrible man. I was glad when he died. Then Mummy was free at last. Oh she cried and cried but it was all crocodile tears for my benefit, just so I'd think she'd loved him. She loved me, not him.

Actually, sitting in that car after the accident was where my interest in bodies began. So I suppose, in a way, I have my father to thank for my career.

There is no doubt in my mind that, before the days when I took courage and found my darlings, I was at my peak of happiness in the midst of an autopsy. People like me are needed, for we are happy doing something that most people would find abhorrent.

Someone has to do it or forensic science would be back in the dark ages, instead of being at the cutting edge as it is today. From my point of view, once you come to understand the beauty of the workings of the human form it becomes a fascination that takes you over. They may be mute but the dead can speak volumes.

My cadavers and I would have long conversations and before parting company for good I would be more familiar with the latter's anatomy than any parent or lover ever would or could have been when they were living.

The biggest regret I have is that earlier in my life, I didn't find the courage to do anything about what I was missing because the best times I ever had were those final days spent with my darlings. The best days ever. Those beautiful people whom I could love without the horrible business of sex ruining the purity of what we had.

Oh, but when I recall the times that I spent with them, the love that I felt – those blissful feelings, such feelings! I got to know them so very well. First meeting them, the intensity of which is hard to describe. It was just beautiful. How much I miss them.

Killing them was far from enjoyable, although being close to them was ecstatic and holding them close was wonderful... indeed, there were a few moments when I wanted to hang on to them alive just to feel them next to me. But they had to go. Of course they did. And then, removing and carrying home so carefully the parts of them that I would keep forever to remember them by. Well, that was a sensation I could never describe.

And knowing I would see the darlings again so soon was such a delicious feeling. For shortly their homecomings to the various mortuaries would happen. Once they were home with me then I could really get to know them so, so well. I would get to know them inside out, you could say.

The two of us could have a chance to be properly alone and talk at length to one another in our own special, silent language. What delightful times we spent together. What was so special was that each of them was deeply grateful to me. In their different ways they all told me how liberated they felt to be relieved of the burden of their sexuality. Oh, how I hate that word. Poor angels, until I came along, that component weighed them down in life, dictating their feelings and so often directing them on to the wrong path. At last, through me they were able to find their true selves and I was lucky in that once they knew I was their saviour, together we experienced a profound reciprocal love.

To know that I had something of those darlings with me for always. Parts that would stay close to me in real terms. I mean, that would live with me in my house and that would always be there waiting for me whenever I was at home. And when I was there, I could feel the nearness of them. Oh, how I ache for them, long for them. I miss them so, so much. But their souls are still with me. Always.

For each of my darlings, I chose our own special song. To find someone you love and who loves you back is a good feeling. But when you find a true soulmate, it is a truly great feeling. My darlings are all my soulmates. They understand me like no other could or ever would. They love me like no other could or would. They are all in my heart and are there for me forever, no matter what, as I shall be for them. They say that nothing lasts forever, but I know, that hearts do go on even after we're all gone. That beautiful love song, 'My Heart Will Go On' is the song I sing for all my loves. They each have their own special song but that is the one that is for all of them.

I kept them on the tables as long as I justifiably could and when each one had to leave the parting was almost too painful to bear. When Phoebe was out, which was fortunately more and more, I would go up to the attic and hold the treasured precious parts of whomever I had, just to say goodbye. I would hold and rock them close to my heart and sing them our special songs, sometimes for hours if Phoebe was out for long.

How I wished I didn't have to wear goggles, apron and rubber gloves to feel closer to my darlings but formaldehyde is a nasty chemical and one has to be so careful. Over the years I have thoroughly trained my mind to ignore unpleasant odours so that has never much bothered me.

'The Power of Love', is Winston's song. 'Just the Two of Us' for my dark, handsome Ahmad. Ginger Jim: 'I Will Always Love You'. My pretty Rob is 'Over the Rainbow' and lovely blond Jack, 'You'll Never Walk Alone'.

There is a young psychiatric nurse here who has caught my eye. He's small. Delicate. Quite a fine young person. His name is Michael. I have noticed that he wears a chain round his neck. It is meant to be hidden under his uniform but I have seen glimpses of it from time to time.

He trusts me now. I have managed to smuggle a plastic fork into my cell. They don't trust us with metal cutlery, more's the pity. If I can just grab the necklace from behind, insert the fork and twist it...

No, now come on, Edward, that's just a fantasy... a better plan would be to find something to silently garrotte him with (a strip of sheeting with a carefully tied knot in it, perhaps) then if I did it at the right time in the right place, maybe I could spend some time alone with Michael. I think I may need to gag him beforehand. He definitely needs deactivating, needs to be neutralised, to be made safe for others. All I need is a knife. I'm working on it. I will find one.

In time I know I will. If I can get a plastic one from my food tray and somehow sharpen it. I know there will be a way, for where there's a will, there's always a way and as Mamma used to say, Edward can do anything he puts his mind to...

THE END

ACKNOWLEDGEMENTS

Thank you to the wonderful team at Bloodhound Books for all their help. An especially large hand-clap goes to my extremely patient, encouraging and supportive editor Clare Law whose hard work was invaluable in helping iron out the wrinkles to bring about this book.

A NOTE FROM THE PUBLISHER

Thank you for reading this book. If you enjoyed it please do consider leaving a review on Amazon to help others find it too.

We hate typos. All of our books have been rigorously edited and proofread, but sometimes mistakes do slip through. If you have spotted a typo, please do let us know and we can get it amended within hours.

info@bloodhoundbooks.com

Printed in Great Britain
by Amazon

18747700R00150